NOWHERE TO RUN
NOWHERE TO HIDE

A gun.

It was inconceivable. You didn't bring a gun to church and go after the organist.

She had chosen a ridiculous place to hide. Lying on her side, she was utterly helpless. She could not get up easily and certainly could not get up silently. He had only to walk in and scrutinize the room more carefully and he'd see her feet and hair.

On the other hand, he could be looking in the logical hiding spot first: closets, cabinets, and stage.

She might still have a chance.

But what if she didn't?

SAND TRAP

CAROLINE B. COONEY

AVON
PUBLISHERS OF BARD, CAMELOT, DISCUS AND FLARE BOOKS

SAND TRAP is an original publication of Avon Books. This work has never before appeared in book form.

AVON BOOKS
A division of
The Hearst Corporation
959 Eighth Avenue
New York, New York 10019

First Avon Printing, April, 1983

AVON TRADEMARK REG. U. S. PAT. OFF. AND IN OTHER COUNTRIES, MARCA REGISTRADA, HECHO EN U. S. A.

rinted in the U. S. A.

10   9   8   7   6   5   4   3   2   1

PROLOGUE

SOUTH OF THE BEND in Deep River, the Carolina hills begin to flatten. The roads seem narrower as the lush green growth at the sides of the highway gets thicker. The towns materialize less frequently. And then, abruptly, as if you are falling off, the red clay and the curving roads end, and the sand begins.

The sand is disorienting. There's a temptation to reach into the glove compartment for the map to see if the beach has moved inland 150 miles. Surely surf is pounding just beyond that sandy sweep! But the drive goes on and on, and the beach never materializes.

For several miles the trees by the road are stunted and deformed, perhaps from a forest fire a decade earlier or perhaps dwarfed by the prospect of having to grow in sand. But by the time the first retirement condominiums and golf hotels appear, the roadsides are lined with huge magnolias, magnificent century-old hollies, and venerable live oaks, whose massive limbs and draping leaves make secret places for children to play.

The longleaf pines appear, their stately beauty marking the Sandhills a place apart, as if there should be a sentry where the terrain changes, and a guard there to check passports. Under the longleafs, little dogwoods and young hollies are hung with dropped brown pine needles, as though decorated for some midsummer celebration. The lawns are parks, either springy with a carpet of fallen needles or raked clean to show the white sand in a peculiar mixture of Oriental and subtropical gardening. Where there are grass lawns there are sprinklers, slowly, gently flooding the sidewalks.

Holly Oak is a fall and spring resort. By June the village is enervatingly hot, the grass already desiccated, and many of the specialty shops and tennis outfitters closed until fall. The score of golf courses are still open, though, and people who don't object to heat or aren't afraid of heart failure still leap about the tennis courts in search of better serves. At each ninth hole the Halfway House buffets serve an assortment of salads, cold cuts, and drinks. Outside the Halfway Houses, row after row of little cream-colored golf carts with gaudy fringed sunshades wait to trundle golfers to the next hole. People who tire of sports saunter into the village and peer into the basement antiques shops or sit on one of the teak benches under the hollies to eat double-scoop ice-cream cones.

There is no litter in Holly Oak. It is difficult to be sure whether the people who visit are too uptown to litter or if the villagers built an underground vacuum system when they were setting in the sprinklers for the golf courses. The roads are blacktop, and the sidewalks—there are side-walks everywhere, unusual in the South—are brick, laid in complicated varying patterns. There are no traffic lights; the atmosphere is too leisurely for such constant blinking. Scores of tiny parking lots dot the streets, each handsomely bordered half a century ago with fire thorn, holly, or pine.

The Sandhills villages—Holly Oak, Pinehurst, Southern Pines—seem like toys, to be taken out on special occasions and played with; in summer, like toys relegated to the attic: hot, dusty, and deserted.

They are among the very few southern towns to have the New England habit of enclosure; every house wrapped in its thick glade of shrubs for privacy. Elsewhere in the Carolinas a hedge is considered unneighborly, and a fence an insult permissible only if one plans to harbor savage dogs. In Holly Oak the unspoken conviction is that any dog would be pedigreed, leashed, and civilized.

There are far more narrow roads than seem necessary for a town the size of Holly Oak. Each encompasses a small vista; each is a landscaping adventure in miniature. Yet they all look alike, and it is possible to drive around Holly Oak time and again without detecting one's destination.

It's wise to stay on the blacktop when one drives in the Sandhills. People who casually drive off the roads around Holly Oak probably want sand on their axles.

That is why Kevin was told precisely where to drive. But he hadn't listened. If he were the kind of person who listened, he wouldn't have taken the job to begin with.

And he got stuck in the sand.

CHAPTER
ONE

SATURDAY NIGHT. All it meant to Janney Fraser was that Sunday would arrive in a few more hours.

And God, she thought, do I need a day of rest. The way I feel right now, a broken shoelace would be a crisis.

Her fingers were curled so tightly around her coffee mug it was surprising the china could tolerate the stress. She set it down carefully because what Janney really wanted to do was hurl it across the store and see it splinter.

Her customer, of course, wanted her to play "The Entertainer."

With the possible exception of her own last name, no tune bothered Janney more than Scott Joplin's ragtime. She estimated that in the seventeen months she had had this horrible job she had played "The Entertainer" approximately nine thousand times.

"How can you possibly work with that record shop across the mall blaring out that rock music?" said the customer.

Work? thought Janney. You call this work? This is a prison sentence. "Oh, you get used to it," she lied, beaming. She had trained herself to smile a lot. Huge, toothy grins often leaped erratically about her face. Sometimes she wondered if she looked insane to her customers, or drug-crazed. *I* wouldn't buy from me, that's for sure, she thought. "Now this model," she said, stroking the fake wood surface of the electronic organ her customer was eyeing, "features

9

dialable transposition. It's a wonderful buy right now, too, because—"

"Oh, I'm not buying," said the customer, beaming right back. "I just like to hear you play 'The Entertainer.'"

There were times when Janney thought arthritis would be a blessing.

It was not that she objected to rag or movie themes or fifties' hits. It was the frequency and predictability of the same requests that was annoying. There must have been a thousand good movie themes written since *Dr. Zhivago*, but still, nothing sold organs better than "Lara's Theme." And Janney knew at least a dozen good exuberant rags, but nobody ever wanted anything except "The Entertainer."

That's what I am, she thought: an entertainer. When what I'm supposed to be is a saleswoman.

All 132 of the stores in the mall were having difficulty selling anything, what with inflation and, in the music store's case, the high cost of financing a large item like an organ. Traffic, yes, there was traffic. All over the city the great unmusical unwashed had decided—what with gas prices going up—they were never going anywhere again by car and were coming in demanding hordes to examine home entertainment in the form of electronic organs with built-in tapes, gongs, drums, rhythms, chords, and other assorted abominations.

Unfortunately they were only considering. Not buying.

About nine-thirty an older couple came in. Too late to be serious buyers, or she'd have had them wandering in and out all night. Hymns, probably, Janney thought. She started off with a half-slush, half-rock number by Bill Gaither, moved into Billy Graham's theme song, and closed with a flutey scrap of "Jesu, Joy of Man's Desiring," to add a touch of class. Mr. and Mrs. Simms—they introduced themselves eagerly, always a good sign—listened to her line about how anyone, anyone at all, especially bright people like themselves, could play this little gem in no time, thus finding countless hours of delight at the keyboard. Sure enough, Mrs. Simms found herself poking out the melody to "Rescue the Perishing" and the instrument poked in the chords on its own, and Mr. Simms, standing by, did not seem at all nauseated by the soft swish of brushes on snare drums that automatically accompanied the hymn.

I'm perishing, thought Janney. Rescue me. *Buy.*

But they didn't.

When the Simmses left, she poured herself a ninth cup of coffee. She could no longer tell whether it was life or caffeine making her tremble so much. I don't care what anybody says, Janney thought. It is infinitely nicer to be supported than to do the supporting. And on top of everything else, the owner was leaving her in charge more and more. Don't you understand? she wanted to scream. I have *enough* responsibility. All I want here is a paycheck.

There were some advantages to the job. With the record shop blaring across the mall, she easily kept up with current trends in music. And she didn't have to fret about her baroque technique. She didn't sell to people who knew what *baroque* meant. For a time she'd hung her degree on the wall, but the only person who read it thought a conservatory was a place where you raised plants, so she put the degree back in her attic.

It was ten o'clock. She could close up the store. Janney went through the chores of shutting down with a slight surprise that she was still intact and functioning. The wonderful lack of noise (Janney no longer thought of it as music) was like the end of a long illness.

She kept thinking about Sunday. About resting. Doing nothing. Reviving.

Old acquaintances were hassling her because she wasn't going to church anymore—now when they felt she really needed it. It was difficult to explain that after selling organs six days a week, hearing one a seventh would not be restful.

Everything was locked, unplugged, and turned off. Janney put her right hand on the gray metal knob of the back door of the shop and watched her fingers struggle to turn it. She'd had so much coffee she was perspiring Maxwell

House. She had to get a dustrag from the closest organ bench to dry the knob and her palms and try again.

The public areas of the store were lovely, done in rusty orange, stainless steel, and mirrors, with thick carpets and handsome framed posters. The back room of the store was bare cement and gray block, mops and vacuums propped up like dead people, and a piano bench with one leg snapped off lopsidedly holding an invisible obese musician.

Each of the six ells of the huge shopping mall was wrapped by a ten-foot stucco wall which hid its delivery and garbage areas from the huge parking lots and the public view. By day the courtyard was a grimy sunburned expanse where bits of torn paper fluttered down among the cigarette butts. By night it was Janney's major source of fear.

Not once in a year and a half had she seen anything disturbing in the courtyard. Still, every night, opening the shop door, she found herself peeking, shivering—expecting KKK rally planners or escaped rapists or criminals making dope buys to be waiting for her.

I'm late, Janney thought. I was so tired and dragged out I spent twice as long as I usually do closing up. Everybody will have left by now. I'll be out there alone.

She had allowed her fantasy of the obese musician on the broken bench to get so out of hand that sometimes she was actually afraid to enter the back room for fear of his thick white fingers.

She went swiftly through the back room, let herself into the courtyard, and slammed the door behind her. Its locks clicked firmly into place. Janney stood in the gaudy thin glare of the overhead lights. One of them was about to go out. The bulb buzzed as if preparing to swarm. With a ping like one of the smallest organs (whose "music" always sounded like a series of errors) the light went out. Behind the garbage Dumpsters was nothing now but dark, bulging shadows.

I am tough, Janney said to herself. This is merely a stroll across a vast deserted awful parking lot; it's nothing.

To a woman who has been through what I have been through, a mere bagatelle.

She could not make herself take a single step across the courtyard. To unlock the shop again, go into the mall, and ask a guard to walk her to her car would be admitting defeat.

I admit it, thought Janney. Defeat, thy name is mine.

She put one foot forward, and nothing attacked her, so she forced herself to try it again with the opposite foot.

What really annoyed her was that it was silly to be so afraid. Janney had been sure that repetition and experience would make each of her problems vanish like the tip of a diminuendo sign on a music staff. That her problems would roll down the long V of the decrescendo and disappear. They hadn't. Every single night the same old problems launched themselves at her with the same old ferocity.

She was almost abreast of the Dumpsters and their shadow pits. Courage, courage, she told herself, and nearly bolted from fear when a male voice at her elbow said, "Walk you to your car?"

It was only Todd, kind, pleasant young Todd Weathers, who owned the hobby shop adjacent to the prison where she worked. She wanted so much to be walked to her car that, perversely, it was imperative to go alone. "No, thanks, Todd, I'll be okay. You have a good day?"

"Great sales," said Todd happily, never thinking that she might have been asking after his health. "Best Saturday since December. Everybody seems to be remembering his happy childhood in the Eisenhower years when there was no inflation and we all built model trains in our basements."

Todd was shorter than Janney, at least fifteen years younger, and definitely weighed less. Still, it was good to have his company across the courtyard. Then, of course, she had to face the parking lot itself. Since she arrived at 1:00 P.M., when the lots were full of lunchtime shoppers, her car was all the way across the blacktop next to the highway.

"You really ought to have one of the mall guards walk

you to your car each night, Mrs. Fraser. Especially Saturdays. Somebody might think you had money on you."

She wished Todd wouldn't worry about her. Tediously she had found that other people's worry placed her under an obligation to pacify them. She always had to insist that she was fine, just fine, and so was Ross; yes, everything was under control. The few times Janney had admitted that nothing was fine, least of all with Ross, and control was decades away, her acquaintances had panicked and fled.

"I won't get robbed, Todd. No money. People don't pay for organs. They write a check for the down payment and finance the balance."

"Lots of stupid people in this world, though, Mrs. Fraser. Might figure any purse as fat as that must be full of money."

Even my purse is overweight, she thought drearily.

There were only seven pounds between Janney and the perfect weight, but whenever she was around slim, trim Todd, the pounds seemed to hover and thrust. It wasn't Todd's fault he irked her so much. Once, on a particularly slow day, they'd had dinner together at the Japanese restaurant in the mezzanine. For Janney it was a delightful interlude: She was not Mrs. Fraser, whom Mr. Fraser had left for greener pastures; she was not a serious musician compromised by the need for cash; she was—"You're a liberated matron, aren't you, Mrs. Fraser?" said Todd, attempting a compliment. The vision of herself as a fat swinger on an organ bench ruined the meal.

"Janney," she said, "please just call me Janney."

Liberated matron. She could see this stout, serene, perfectly coiffed creature opening a successful advertising agency, running the bloodmobile campaign, and keeping twenty-four rose bushes sprayed. Me, liberated, she thought. What a joke. All I do is commute between prisons.

"Mrs. Fraser," said Todd.

She could not tolerate that name again. To be stuck with Avery's "Fraser" along with his bills, his house, and his son was tonight beyond bearing. "See you Monday," she said, walking without Todd to her car. Todd stood by the courtyard wall and watched her the whole way. She was grateful to him and annoyed with him, probably just the way he felt toward her. After unlocking the car Janney slid in, locked the door after herself, and sagged with relief. Having slipped off the high heels that had been comfortable at noon and were now gripping her ankles like jaws, she tugged on sports socks and torn white sneakers.

Sunday tomorrow. Rest. Oh, God.

She held her hair back from her face as though brushing away bad nerves and started the engine.

Janney knew the roads so well she drove by memory.

Vaguely she recognized that her inattention was dangerous, but since she kept to small back roads with virtually no traffic, she felt it didn't matter. It took her an hour and thirty minutes to get home, a time she filled by thinking vacantly of the yard, the peonies that needed staking, and the porch paint that was peeling.

Every night Ross would ask suspiciously if she'd gone by the major highways, and every night she would reassuringly lie that of course she had. But on the highway, when she was trying to enjoy the only solitude of her whole week, headlights glared in her mirrors and strangers crowded her. She needed the lonely narrow back roads.

How funny of Todd to think somebody might rob me, Janney thought, when I've been robbed of everything that counts.

Janney Fraser drove down the winding hills of Deep River Road toward Holly Oak, seeing nothing, hearing nothing, filled with the memories of all that she had lost.

CHAPTER
TWO

GREY RANDALLMAN was at the symphony board meeting. They were in the Trustees' Room at the bank, where all civic groups met. He had never been on the symphony board before, although he'd done everything else in Holly Oak and had been somewhat astonished to learn that there were thirty-six people on the board. Grey wouldn't have said there were that many people in the whole county who cared enough about symphonic music to sponsor it. This judgment was confirmed when only nine others, rather furtively, appeared for the meeting. Perhaps the missing twenty-six had been in the Trustees' Room before and didn't care for the atmosphere, which was neither Sandhills stately nor symphonic, but more like a stale airline terminal.

There were no introductions. Everyone who was a resident in Holly Oak knew each other. Grey, as the sole factory owner at this end of the county, was well known because the waitresses and caddies who wintered at the resorts liked to work summers in his mill. Not that there were any waitresses and caddies on the board.

John David opened the meeting. "Y'all know how the symphony works," he said, and a Christmas-tree smile leaped off his teeth. John David worked for every philanthropic organization in town, but the bank paid his salary, which Grey thought very civic-minded of them. He per-

17

sonally liked his employees to contribute to his business, not other people's.

Grey confessed that he did not know how the symphony worked.

"Simple," said John David. "We raise enough cash, and the symphony comes out here to the boondocks and gives us a concert."

"If y'all thought it was hard work integrating the schools," said Sarah, on Grey's left, "you just wait till y'all try selling symphony tickets."

"I sell tickets?" said Grey weakly. That was one of the rules by which he governed his civic existence: Never get tangled up with anything that involves ticket, lottery, or doughnut sales.

"A volunteer to be our ticket chairman!" cried John David. "Wonderful, Grey! Thank you!"

There was a mixture of laughter and mock congratulations, everybody obviously hoping Grey would not take advantage of parliamentary procedure and refuse. Grey shrugged. He'd gotten off the vestry this year and finished up his library board term, so he might as well take on the symphony. They all cheered—not for Grey, but in celebration of not having to run ticket sales themselves.

"So who's going to be guest artist this year?" said Celia. She was a very thin woman, the sort that considers herself elegant, and liked to think she could maintain her elegance in old jeans and too-large men's shirts. She couldn't.

"Giovanni Piero," said John David.

"Don't be silly," said Sarah. "I heard him when I was in my teens. He's bound to be dead by now."

"I surely hope not," said John David. "Though we might sell more tickets that way."

The symphony board met only two or three times a year, at the last minute and with much grumbling. They were meeting Saturday because John David had to get a response into Raleigh by Monday and he really couldn't postpone the meeting much longer. "So, Grey," said John David, "you're responsible for thirty-three hundred dollars. Think you can do it?"

"Did they do it last year?"

There was some dispute over this. Last year's membership chairpeople were conspicuously absent.

"Aw, forget last year," said John David. "The symphony came, so we must've raised the money."

"Did it come?" said Celia. "I wasn't able to attend."

It turned out no one had been able to attend. They weren't really sure if there had been a concert or not. There was a burst of hysterical laughter. "For whom are we organizing this great cultural event anyway?" said Grey. "Obviously not for ourselves."

"For the visitors," said John David, in a voice like a mortician hovering over the remains. *Visitor* was a word used reverently in the Sandhills. A tourist was a vacant-headed dude with a camera around his neck and a bag of foil-wrapped cheeseburgers in his hand. Holly Oak had never had a tourist and never planned to. They had visitors. Visitors who played golf and tennis, shot skeet, ate dinner out, bought trendy sports clothes, stocked up on Christmas presents, and decorated their winter houses in locally stocked designer fabrics.

Grey was swept by a deep affection for his fellow board members, for his town, for this silly job selling tickets to a concert only visitors would care about. And one they'd attend not for the music, but to display themselves, peacocks and peahens in the Holly Inn Pavilion.

"We've also got problems with our extra cash," said John David. "The way it works is, we buy a concert and they don't care how many people show up. So if we sell more tickets than the concert cost us, that money's ours. Now I've been putting it in a savings account, but Raleigh claims to have changed its by-laws and says the money's theirs."

Raleigh was a useful word. In this case it meant the central symphony board. *Raleigh* in other contexts meant taxes, urban blight, bureaucracy, or, occasionally, civilization.

"How is everyone in Raleigh anyway?" said Sarah. Seventy-eight and white haired, she was at one time the piano teacher of everybody in this room, including Grey, who could still remember the fingering on the first Clementi sonatina.

"Hospitalized," said John David. "Or insane. I don't think it's been a banner year for them."

Grey found himself wondering what Sarah and John David and Celia would think of what he and Kevin were doing that night. What he would think of himself later. He would be committing the first definitely illegal act of his entire fifty-six years.

He shrugged. He hadn't been able to afford the poison waste transfer firm. A hundred sixty-five dollars a barrel, just to truck his trash away? Ridiculous! The stuff had been okay there in the back of the factory. Damn inspectors, hounding him about retroactive regulations and safety standards. Let them find $165,000 to move the stuff.

"Look at all these patrons," said Celia, studying last year's donor list. "Hamburger chains, plumbers, landscapers. I see that my star visitors would fit alphabetically between a peach warehouse and a funeral home."

"As I recall," said John David, "your visitors do have the brains of peach pits."

"True. But they pay vastly for the use of my guest cottage."

Everyone agreed that this more than compensated for a lack of intelligence.

The phone rang. John David picked it up. "Holly Oak Bank and Trust," he said melodiously, as if it were Monday morning at nine instead of late Saturday night. "Sure, just a sec."

He handed the phone to Grey.

Nobody spoke. They shared the squirrelly curiosity of the small town; the complete conviction that anything going on anywhere was surely their business, too. Grey's voice filled the quiet room. "Hello?"

"Sorry to bother you, dear," said his wife, "but Kevin called on the truck telephone. Says he has to talk to you. Something's gone wrong. He really sounded quite urgent, Grey."

Grey's fingers, wrapped around the receiver, went cold and numb, as if frostbitten. There was a sharp, stabbing pain in his shoulders, and for one choking instant he thought of heart attacks.

But it was just fear.

Oh, my God, he thought. Why did I have Kevin in on this? He never listens. That crazy self-centered fool. What's he done now? What's gone wrong?

"Okay," he said into the phone. "Probably nothing, Catherine. Don't worry. See you shortly."

He did not offer to explain this conversation to the other board members, and they, reluctantly, did not press.

"How much do you have to give to be a patron?" said Celia.

"Honey, a donor is one who donates. Give and ye shall be listed," said John David.

And on the last of the trips, too, thought Grey. There's a jinx on Kevin. He's a loser decked out in winner's ribbons.

"There's no minimum?" said Sarah.

Grey had a solid presentiment that whatever Kevin had done was not going to be a peccadillo. If it had been, Kevin would have weaseled out of it without mentioning it to anybody, least of all to Grey. It was going to be something totally, irrevocably, irretrievably wrong.

"Not to me," said John David. "Course, Raleigh wants a minimum." His voice implied that anyone residing at the state capital was suspect in all desires. "But I say, screw the old by-laws. We didn't vote on 'em."

The pain in his chest subsided, but now Grey seemed to have fear pulsing out of his heart. "Listen, something's come up," he said. "I'll call you Monday about the ticket sales, John David."

"Sure, Grey, fine."

He left the room with difficulty. The babble continued like a cartoon strip running on page after page. Grey had the most horrifying sensation that he was leaving his life behind in that room.

CHAPTER
THREE

I'VE FINISHED PLAYING WITH MY TOYS, thought Ross bitterly. It's nap time. He tried to make himself smile and failed. To be thirty and have to play with toys. God.

He turned off his lights and stared out into the yard. It was an acre and a half, completely enclosed by thick shrubbery and leaning oaks. The two neighbors were winter visitors who sensibly spent the summers in Kennebunkport and Nantucket, so no lights came from those houses. There was nothing to see except stars and a full moon, and astronomy was one of the few hobbies Ross had never taken up.

Ross often wanted to suggest to Janney that they move. The unchanging sight of the grass scrap he could not mow, the heavenly bamboo he could not prune, the sandy driveway he could not grade made his limp muscles ache. And he did not know how Janney could stand it, every day seeing the yard where Donny had played, the trees Donny had climbed.

A high-rise apartment over some busy city, he thought. Now that would be good. Boston maybe. Janney loves Boston. Demolition and construction gangs to watch, or maybe street gangs, or police breaking up street gangs. Boats docking or planes landing.

But what the other side of the house faced was the golf course.

The local style in housing was to sprinkle the single-family and attached homes around the golf courses, so each picture window faced a fairway or studied a green. The house Avery Fraser had bought was on a cul-de-sac (realtors could ask 10 percent more for a house on a cul-de-sac, whereas a house on a dead end did nothing for the price at all), and beyond its yard, a narrow wood, and a wide strip of rough sat the third hole of one of Holly Oak Country Club's six courses.

Ross had never been attracted to golf, but hundreds of visitors spent every day of the year conquering these little green worlds. To Ross, the players resembled trained chimpanzees, learning to use primitive sticklike tools, never quite catching up to the ball they'd been sent after. Very few walked. Ross kept a bird list. Sometimes he felt the walking golfer was rare enough to deserve notation on such a list. Mostly they sat in tiny electric carts with gay fringed sunshades, steering themselves from fallen ball to fallen ball. The carts emitted low-pitched, robotlike whirs, and Ross liked the carts much better than the ritualized people who hopped in and out of them.

He was mechanical. In his teens nothing of Ross's had ever broken down because he had a constant and satisfying program of preventive maintenance. More than anything it galled him to hear the choking rattle of Janney's car. He had tried working on the Pinto from the wheelchair, but he couldn't reach things and, unable to get above the engine, lacked the leverage necessary to unbolt or pry or tighten. They'd tried having Ross tell Janney what to do, but she was convinced she had the hot wire confused with the ground wire and was about to get a fatal shock, and when he finally did get her to put the wrench on the right bolt, she couldn't get the nut off.

The Pinto was in terrible shape, a not uncommon problem with Pintos. They'd replaced the transmission, and it had a new battery and a new fuel pump; but now it needed a valve job, new shocks, new brake linings, and God knew what else. They lacked the money to have somebody else fix it, and with all the driving Janney did, it was simply dangerous.

Ross did not bother to lower the hospital bed. He could never sleep until Janney was home. It shamed him. He told himself it was worry for her that kept him awake— that he was the fuddy-duddy parent with a wayward teenager who couldn't be trusted to stay on the highway—but basically he hated being alone. Besides, the only thing he could contribute to any endeavor now was worry, so he worried.

If that car breaks down, he thought, Janney will break down, too.

He closed his eyes against the thought of Janney's collapsing. An actual thread of fear went through him, and he had to clutch the wide hem of the cotton sheet to steady himself. It was a familiar infuriating gesture.

Macho man Ross Fraser, he thought derisively. Whither goest?

Goest to the veterans hospital if Janney cracks up.

Janney's ability to deal with problems had withered away. Yesterday when the toaster got stuck, he'd found her weeping over it. It had been a good morning for Ross, he'd been up and wheeling around, and he felt like a knight of the Round Table unplugging the toaster and rescuing the English muffin. He even got her to laugh about it, and for a rare moment it was Ross restoring Janney's equilibrium instead of the other way around. But that morning she went out to rake up the hundreds of brown crackling magnolia leaves that were littering the yard, and about three-quarters of the way through the job—a simple enough task Ross would have given anything to do himself—the tines fell off her rake handle. All Janney needed was a screw, but she simply left the two halves of the rake in the yard and walked unsteadily away.

He could see the tines now, winking in the moonlight.

Sometimes Ross looked at Janney, so tired and burned out, and he wanted to cry out with apologies, tell her he was sorry, he hadn't meant to be a burden to anybody, that his life plans had included being a basketball coach and getting a commercial pilot's license.

But he never told Janney anything because the times

he most wanted not to be a burden were the humiliating times, when she was checking the catheter or changing the sheets, and then he was filled with anger at her, for being whole, for being stronger, and mobile, and female.

He was her duty in life.

Ross did not think anything could be worse than being someone else's chore.

Kevin saw the deer in his headlights as he was taking the curve, and the desire to shoot it was so strong he could think of nothing else. He'd lost his hunting license after that little thing with Rory last November, and he hadn't had a chance to use his guns in months—long, dry, wasted months—and here he was on a back road at night and no one would know and it was a deer; he loved hunting deer.

Not that there was much of a hunt involved. He finished the curve and drove the heavy truck right up into the sand, twisting the wheel hard, so he could find the deer again with his headlights. He drove almost into the pines, and there were its eyes, colored like Christmas ornaments, trapped by his lights. Kevin slipped out of the cab and waited as long as he could before shooting, savoring the moment, stroking the rifle.

Everyone Kevin knew hunted to be out of doors, to display expertise with a gun, to enjoy the woods. Kevin hunted to kill. A few years back he had dated a girl who thought hunting was "absolutely revolting, Kevin, how can you *do* it?" Kevin could no more have done without hunting than without food or sex or sleep. He believed that killing was a basic human need. Why else would there be these politically senseless wars through the millennia? Hunters were the only sane people. No sublimation of primary needs for them. That was why you had all this child abuse and wife beating. Not enough hunting.

Kevin shot. There was a familiar moment of suffocating excitement as the bullet left his gun and sped through the air and made its soft entry into softer flesh; the old hot pleasure coursed through Kevin when he ran up to see the blood pulse out the bullet hole and body quiver as life left it.

A doe.

It was a good thing his uncle Grey would never find out about this. Grey would rant and rave about helpless fawns and how the deer population would be destroyed by Kevin alone if Kevin kept up this evil slaughter. He'd demand to know how Kevin happened to have a loaded rifle in the truck with him anyway. And he'd bring up the whole annoying thing of Rory's death.

Rory's death, he had told the authorities, was an accident. But the police had plagued him with questions for months. How could you have hit him? He was wearing an orange jacket. He was shot from close range. How could you have mistaken him for a deer? How come you didn't carry him to help? Or run for help yourself? How come you spent an hour trying to revive Rory when you were only a few hundred yards from a well-trafficked road?

More than half a year ago that had happened, and still, every time he went into the village one of those stupid cops sauntered over as if he owned the bricks in the sidewalk and brought it up again. Kevin often thought that if he had felt good killing Rory, he'd feel wonderful killing a cop.

Rory had been slow to die. He'd gurgled and patted the ground and rolled his eyes and clutched at the air. And at the end his throat had rattled. Kevin could hear the sound now. It was unlike anything else he'd ever heard.

For one last satisfying moment Kevin looked down at his dead doe. Pity he couldn't haul the deer home for the venison. But he had no plastic bags, no knives, and no freezer to hide it in from prying relatives' eyes. Grey was too damn law-abiding, that was it.

Kevin would have preferred not to work for his uncle. Kevin was sure the only way Grey could bring himself to dispose of the poison wastes like this was Grey's conviction that he wasn't really doing anything wrong; it was the situation that was impossible. He would have preferred not to work at all, but his parents wouldn't let him live at home if he didn't. He couldn't live alone because then a lot of his money would have to go to maintaining a household instead of into sports and cars and clothes. And he'd seen what people had to go through when they lived alone. All that laundry and shopping and cooking. Eventually you had to clean the bathroom. Kevin, who was fastidious, would much prefer to have his mother do it than find himself scouring the stupid tile. His friends got so tired of all the housekeeping garbage they married, but marriage hardly ever turned out to be a passport to clean clothes and good food. Instead, it was an open door to whining babies, who were the ones who ended up with the clean clothes and the good food.

Gently Kevin set the rifle in the cab and pulled himself up after it. He never did physical things without noticing himself doing them. Even the act of getting into a vehicle was a moment for self-admiration. Kevin enjoyed his long, lean, tanned body, the tough thrust of the muscles below the cutoff wheat jeans as he swung his legs in. Kevin did not notice the torn vinyl upholstery or the wadded-up dirty Kleenex the last driver had thrown on the floor. He saw his own arms, his long, firm, capable fingers and the brown paper bag from the gun shop. He opened the bag and drew out a new box of shells. A plastic film encased the cardboard. The untouched readiness of the shell boxes was as satisfying a sight to Kevin as an unopened book to a reader or a new set of crayons to a child.

He fondled the boxes, thinking of windowpanes and woodchucks. He didn't feel like emptying the gun. There was a sense of incompleteness, of an important job not yet accomplished, when you took out the shells you'd intended to fire. Loading a gun was fun. Emptying it was a chore.

Hauling the company waste products was enough of a chore already.

Kevin checked the safety on the rifle and decided to take the risk of traveling with it. A state trooper might stop a pickup truck whose driver was drunkenly weaving all over the road, but he doubted they'd glance at the liquid carrier of Holly Oak Industries.

Kevin put the truck in neutral. Its engine was exceptionally noisy. He loved noise, and he shoved the accelerator to make a good roar. Primeval, he thought. He wished he could hunt bear and walrus and elephant instead of lousy old rabbits and deer. Someday, thought Kevin, someday I'll hunt something more exciting.

He revved the engine several times just to hear the lionlike roar. Then he slammed the gears into reverse.

The sand sucked up his wheels as easily as a child sucks soda up a straw. The truck never went backwards at all; it simply sank, its huge wheels hurling sand away by the shovelful, as if digging graves.

He couldn't believe it. How could this have happened to him? Goddamn sand, he thought savagely, leaping out of the cab. Goddamn truck. Goddamn Grey.

He'd never be able to move the truck. It was too heavy by tons. Rage swept through Kevin. Grey was always ruining things for Kevin. Always placing demands. Always work, work, work. Saturday *night,* for Christ's sake. It was Grey's fault, choosing Saturday night. Kevin got Aunt Catherine on the radiotelephone and chewed her out some, usually a turn-on because she got so stiff and elegant on him, but this time it eased nothing.

He didn't care about the poison or the long, expensive job that would be involved extricating the truck. He cared about his hunting license. They'd find that deer and he'd never get another license, and he couldn't stand it, not being able to hunt another year. Kevin took the tire iron and began hitting the sides of the truck to get some of the wrath out of his muscles.

It gave him an idea. A terrific idea. He began laughing with delight. "Kid, you're smart," he whispered to himself. "You're a smart bastard, all right."

Catherine Randallman was from Messina, New York, a town for which one adjective may always be reliably applied: *cold.* In Catherine's opinion, North Carolina was unhealthy. For one reason: the heat. She firmly believed that people as well as apple trees needed a period of dormancy, a good chill on the bones to cleanse out illness and stiffen the spine.

Some New Englander had founded Holly Oak in 1915 as a convalescent center. The old rest homes were still there, full of residents, though presumably a new set. And they rested. Did they ever rest. Catherine spent half of every day, Monday through Friday, jostling elderly, confused widows out of bed and trying to convince them that activity was better than rest. She'd been at it for years, and every morning when she got there, they all were still hanging around on their beds, resting. It was enough to make a woman surrender.

She was thinking of getting a paying job. Grey was complaining a good deal about money now, and she was no sponge, not one of these lazy natives who started resting at about age twenty-two and merely increased in proficiency every year.

She didn't really want to change her routine, though. She loved her life just the way it was. In fact, Catherine Randallman had only two regrets about her existence. One, that the children had chosen northern New York in which to live. Sensible, and certainly what she had steeped them in, but nevertheless, it made visiting difficult. And as sure as she decided to retire back up there, they'd decide to move down here.

The other regret was Grey's half sister's son Kevin.

If you asked Catherine, and Grey often nervously did, Kevin was not playing with a full deck.

He didn't look it. He was a typical country club golden boy, right down to the fair hairs on his deeply tanned arms and the toothpaste ad smile decorating his handsome face. He always looked as if he had just left a hairstylist. Catherine thought he had a blow dryer at every locker location, very likely one in his car, so he could always look perfect. Kevin perceived himself as perfect.

If it were mere conceit, Catherine could have accepted it. She had a pretty large ego herself. But Kevin surpassed conceit and entered a sort of Nixonian zone in which he,

Kevin, could do no wrong because by definition what Kevin did was perfect.

There was a much-bandied-about saying in sports: Winning isn't important, it's everything.

Catherine had never known a person who took this as much to heart as Kevin. Like the local Jaycee who kept $50,000 in charity money from the grape jelly sale and went right on pretending to be a good citizen, Kevin did not feel bad about his cheating at sports because he, Kevin, had done it, and he, Kevin, was perfect.

Catherine had played golf with Kevin once.

Throughout the game, Kevin watched her with the intensity of a starving animal waiting its turn at the food.

Catherine had made a hole in one, a perfect shot, the sort when she'd felt the triumph even as her eyes followed the arc of the ball. She'd lost sight of it in the air and glued her eyes to the soft plush green and she was half laughing with delight, and Kevin growled.

Growled like a dog.

Like the time they had to put the old collie to sleep and Kevin said to the vet, "I'll do it," and he took the needle out of the vet's hand and was trembling with excitement. Kevin gripped old Punch's fur and exposed the flesh, and his lips moved back to expose his teeth, and Catherine, numb and shocked, thought Kevin looked more like a canine than Punch did, with his fangs exposed like that. And it wasn't Punch that growled; it was *Kevin,* with a terrible bright pleasure seeping out of his mouth as he forced the killing fluid into his own dog's body. At the end the dog convulsed, not much, not horribly, but a little, and Kevin writhed with him, and Kevin's hand was not soothingly stroking his dog into a final peace: Kevin's hand was rubbing his crotch.

If Catherine had not seen that, she could have erased the whole episode from her memory. But the dog's death had aroused Kevin. Sometimes she thought about Rory and wondered if during that—if at the very moment that Rory—but she had to put that out of her mind because it was too horrible to think of Rory's dying and Kevin with his hands in his pants, enjoying it.

And Catherine was afraid. Afraid of her own nephew, on a lovely sunny day when the laughter of other twosomes drifted across the grass, because she was winning and Kevin could not bear to have other people win. Afraid of how his lips pulled back and he took on that faint doglike look, and how his hands closed tightly around the shaft of the golf club, she found her thoughts going back to Punch and Rory. When she made the hole in one, she said, "Just wild luck, Kevin, I couldn't do that again in a million years," and on purpose she fumbled everything for the rest of the game.

It gave Catherine a sick feeling in her stomach to talk to Kevin. They had stuck by Kevin during the Rory thing because that was what families were for, sticking by, but all the time Catherine wondered if maybe something in Kevin would stick to her as well.

Grey and Kevin were up to something. Grey had been tense when they left, and Kevin amused. Nothing Kevin laughed at amused Catherine. She suppressed a shudder.

It was eleven-thirty, and Grey had not missed the eleven o'clock news since their last child was born. What was he doing? Was he doing it with Kevin?

Grey and Catherine had an evening ritual: television news; complaining about the news; calming each other down; sex; sleep. Catherine was very fond of the entire sequence. Except for the news. She could have done without that.

She phoned his office at the mill. The switchboard was closed, of course, but if he were there, he'd answer his own line.

No one answered.

The symphony board members had long since deserted the bank.

She tried to raise Kevin again on the truck's radio-telephone but got no response. The little gadget had a small range. Had Kevin driven on, somewhere beyond range? Or was he no longer in the truck? No longer near the phone? And Grey? Where was he?

Catherine opened the bedroom curtains so she could watch the driveway for the red Cadillac.

CHAPTER

FOUR

THERE WAS NO TRAFFIC on Deep River Road. People driving to Holly Oak and Southern Pines and Pinehurst didn't want a scenic route; they wanted to get there and play a few holes of golf before dark. And there was little local traffic because there were very few locals living along the way.

At midnight the road belonged to Janney.

She read the signs. The Civitans welcomed her to Acorn Ridge. Joe Patrick's Bobwhite Quail Farm was not open on Sundays. Case was running for state auditor. First Baptist was a going church for a coming Savior.

She passed the lake which smelled as if it were fermenting and the yard that sported dead trees hung with hollowed-out gourds where presumably bluebirds lived in companionable colonies. The next landmark was the house whose owners had bordered their immense circular drive with white painted tires, each cut to resemble giant flower petals. Every few miles Janney passed a house with a school bus parked in its drive, except this trip the buses were gone. She had developed a long fantasy about the notorious school bus thief when she realized that school was over and the buses were probably stored for the summer in some fenced-in lot.

The first longleaf pine appeared.

Janney had never liked them. They looked like warped telephone poles with skin-cancer-like bark. The dark sparse branches with their lean crop of needles looked like normal pine trees going through a famine.

They'd come to Holly Oak because Avery wanted to play golf year round. Janney didn't play. Ross couldn't.

She detested Holly Oak. It was a precious town, a distillation of all cute New England villages in narrow rocky valleys, but Holly Oak's darling, purposely crowded byways looked stupid to Janney when beyond them the Sandhills stretched in all directions.

Southern Pines was much nicer, a town that had grown instead of being planned. She'd tried to find a good job in Southern Pines, but it was the sort of place where you were supposed to bring wealth with you, not acquire it. Thus the mall, the drive, and the exhaustion at the end of each day.

Now there was enough sand to catch in her headlights. Drifts of it here and there and the distinctive ridge of white sand that for a quarter mile rimmed the road. This was where she always pretended to be arriving at the beach for a holiday. The pretense was helped along by the rank, low-tide scent of a nearby pig farm.

The drive seemed twice as long as usual.

I'm not going to be able to keep this up, Janney thought. Everybody is right after all. They told me I'm no superwoman, and I'm not. I'm a loser. Ross is a loser. We're a matched pair.

She'd been organist at an Episcopal church for a while where the rector had a very Baptist idea of sermon length and no standards whatsoever about lucidity. Since the organ was exposed, Janney felt she had to make a pretense of listening, although she'd have preferred to do needlework or read the Sunday paper. Instead, she opened the Book of Common Prayer on the music ledge and changed the page every week. After reading them through fifty times in a row, Janney got to know a lot of psalms very well. Put my tears in your bottle, God, she thought. Record them in your book. For darkness is my only companion.

Janney considered herself an atheist. It was clear to her that if God had any power, He was using it sloppily and prejudicially. On the other hand, Janney often needed someone to talk to, and invariably God was the only one around.

Ross, of course, was there.

Two years ago they'd enjoyed each other. She had even thought, for a while, that Ross would survive after all, would come up smiling. But after Donny and Avery, Ross had stiffened until now he was about as flexible as peanut brittle. There were times when their most meaningful conversations dealt with the amount of sugar that should be added to the iced tea.

God, said Janney, for the millionth time, on the off chance that there might be one and He might be listening and willing to help Ross.

Religious people were the whole trouble with church work. She'd get an organ job Sunday no matter how tired she was of organs, for the money, but there were always religious people hovering around in churches, and Janney could not stand them.

She stopped the car to get out and carry a box turtle across the road before it got smashed by a wheel. Box turtles always knew where they were going, an admirable trait, so she carefully faced it in the same direction on the opposite side of the road.

Back in the car she sighed, and sighed again. It did not seem to be a rejuvenating exercise, and finally she put the car in gear and drove on.

Grey had known that Kevin was stupid. But getting that heavy truck caught in the sand! Grey hadn't thought he was that stupid. And certainly it would never have crossed Grey's mind that it would seem logical to Kevin to lighten the truck by dumping the poison, thereby making it easier to get out of the sand.

Grey stared at the sand. It was so porous that literally ten minutes after a Noah's Ark deluge, a person could walk over the sand and not get the soles of his shoes wet. Nice attribute in an area where golf was king. The chamber of commerce mentioned it twice in every publication.

Now, in the space where his car's headlights pointed, Grey could see pools of ruddy orange and black goo percolating into the ground.

Dear Christ, thought Grey. Where is it going? Underground streams? Somebody's well water? A branch of Deep River?

The stench was overwhelming.

Grey could not move, could not think. It was complicated by the chest pain. He must have pulled a muscle playing tennis.

At the factory he'd kept the inevitable poisonous wastes stored in tanks. The factory produced less than a half ton a month, and it had never seemed much of a problem to Grey. Whenever the tanks were full, he'd haul the muck up to some worthless red clay acreage he owned in Randolph County and fill in ditches with it. It had been a perfectly logical and legal way to clear the poison, and it wasn't till the last year or so that Grey grasped from the national media there was anything wrong with this disposal technique.

Poison was a subject as taboo as homosexuality had once been. You acknowledged that poisons were produced elsewhere, but not where you lived. Certainly not if you lived in Holly Oak, the perfect retirement village.

And this place, right here, where Kevin was stuck was not Grey's property. He did not know who owned this land or what it was used for.

Have to notify someone, he thought. Who? Police? FBI? Environmental Protection Agency? Or just my friendly local garbage man?

I, Grey Randallman, civic mainstay of Holly Oak, am poisoning the countryside of the Sandhills. Making a little Love Canal. Schoolchildren probably stand here to catch their bus. Pregnancies probably start in that grove of trees. The peaches in the orchard over there probably end up on the president's fruit salad plate.

Grey leaned against his car. He was astonished at how weak he was from the shock of Kevin's stupidity. He had

handled enough crises by now. All he had to do was pull
himself together and handle this one.

But both mind and body seemed to fade away.

The per barrel removal fee had been staggering, even
if he'd kept the poison in convenient barrels, and he hadn't.
The fee was even higher for basic cleanup operations. And
the only firm Grey could locate that even handled toxic
wastes had had such adverse publicity over *its* disposal
techniques that Grey could not bear the thought of his
company's name linked to it in one of the now more fre-
quent newspaper articles.

So Grey decided to dispose of the current overload of
waste in the same way he always had, but by night and
without discussion, because this time he did know the
regulations and the environmental problems. Nobody was
aware of his Randolph County dump site.

Well, he'd cheated, and he was caught.

What was Catherine going to think about him? What
would his town think? God, what was going to happen
next?

Grey swallowed a sick feeling.

He eyed his stupid nephew. Look on the bright side.
This might develop the boy's character. Strength through
adversity and all that. "Well, kid," he said, "we're in trouble now." He felt slightly less horrified after expressing
his fears aloud. "I don't even know who's going to have to
be in on this. Start with the police, I guess."

"The police?" said Kevin. *"The police?"*

The pain in Grey's chest repeated itself. With a knowledge cold and grim as rain, he realized this was no pulled
muscle, no frisson of fear.

He was having a heart attack.

Ross was thirsty. The aide who came in the afternoons
had fixed him a thermos of lemonade, but he'd finished it.
He couldn't even remember the woman's name. Aides came
and went with depressing rapidity.

He reached for the pull rope he used to ease himself off
the bed and into his wheelchair, but just reaching for the

rope exhausted him. It was one of those nights when he felt so weak his body melted into the mattress; he was a corpse attending his own wake.

Pity I'm not, Ross thought.

The pain, like the past, was intractable.

Donny had discovered carpentry shortly before his fifth birthday. Glorying in what a hammer could do with a nail, Donny built wooden crossing signs to help people, he explained, wanting to cross the yard. Being a nonreligious four-year-old who didn't ride trains, Donny didn't know the difference between a *T* cross and an *X* cross, so he nailed his crossing signs vertically. The yard resembled nothing so much as a revival camp waiting for the tent and preacher.

The crosses turned out to be omens.

Ross turned the radio on to get his mind off his little brother. He tried a dozen stations before giving up. He was not in a listening mood.

He wondered where Janney was by now. Coleridge, maybe. Peter had driven him up there once. A narrow dark curve where enormous trees hovered over huge empty mills, vines filling the broken glass of the old windows and truck bodies waiting for the delivery that would never come. What possessed Janney to drive through twilight zones like Coleridge when she could go sensibly down 220 he'd never know.

If only he still had Peter.

Peter came the year Donny was born. Twenty years old and an aspiring tennis pro, Peter would come by at odd hours to help with Ross. Peter had a van, to which he'd carry Ross as easily as Janney carried Donny and plunk him down on the raised mattress in the rear. From the peculiar assortment of custom windows—round, heart-shaped, fleur-de-lis—Ross watched whatever Peter felt like parking near: deserted mills, tennis lessons for a weight watchers' group, horses being trained for dressage at Holly Oak Stables, or swim meets for nine-year-olds at the Holly Inn outdoor pool.

Peter had given him terrific back rubs. He'd also tried

all sorts of Oriental pressure point theories to assuage his headaches, written letters to physicians at pain centers, convinced Janney to experiment with vegetarian and vitamin regimens to clear up his vertigo. None of this achieved much, but the sense of trying, the knowledge that somebody besides his stepmother cared got Ross through another year.

It was Peter who forced Ross to learn code and get his ham license. Peter who got the binoculars and bird manuals and weather guides. Peter who arranged the bookmobile visits, started the magazine subscriptions, found good radio talk shows from Tel Aviv to New York, got Ross addicted to the one-thirty soap opera instead of to aspirin, and did crosswords and anagrams with him.

But then Peter was offered a tennis job at a country club near Sea Island in Georgia, and that was that.

Ross thought of being put back in the veterans hospital. Of his bedroom stripped. His tools and toys and machines, everything that made the time between sleeps bearable, packed in boxes. Boxes for which there might or might not be room in a hospital ward.

He looked at the clock. Another half hour before Janney'd be home.

Ross lay on the mattress as tense as if it were Vietnam again and he could expect the roof to be bombed while she was gone.

Kevin could not believe his uncle was serious. "Grey," he protested, "nobody's seen this. In a minute it will all soak in and we can rake it over with pine needles, and nobody's going to know."

All the sports Kevin liked required long, thin tools. He stroked them, relishing the habit as a pipe smoker does tamping the tobacco. Golf clubs, tennis rackets, baseball bats, riding crops. Only soccer didn't take equipment; it used his elbows, head, and thighs. At first he felt silly in soccer. When his team began to win, though (Kevin followed Will Rogers's stock-market advice about winning:

Play on a winning team—if it don't win, don't play), Kevin found he liked soccer, too.

He found himself reaching for his rifle. Infants reached for pacifiers. Kevin reached for one of the tools that always made him a winner. "The stuff doesn't matter, Grey," he said.

His uncle said something about civic duty. About how admitting one's errors promptly prevented one from falling into the Nixonian trap. About facing the music.

A deer shot out of season began to seem minor.

They put you in prison for dumping poisons, didn't they? Or was it just a fine? Kevin tried to remember the outcome of the trial of those New Jersey men who'd been caught dumping in Halifax County.

He had a good friend who'd been into cigarette smuggling for years. North Carolina had low state taxes on cigarettes; New York, high taxes. There was a nice profit in the difference, or had been before gasoline cost so much. R2D2 (Roy Delphia, Jr., who got his nickname from a much brighter girl friend after they'd seen *Star Wars* eleven times) felt the income was well worth the risks. Like sports, R2D2 said to Kevin, your team has to beat. Exciting.

But R2D2's team lost an inning, and R2D2 had a longer number now because the state police caught him just over the Virginia border.

Kevin loathed cops.

The six he'd reluctantly gotten to know on the Holly Oak force (some force, thought Kevin) pranced around in their cute little short-sleeved uniforms as if they practiced tennis lobs at their police academy instead of frisking.

"Call the cops?" he said to his uncle.

He'd gone to see R2D2 just once at the prison. The music R2D2 faced turned out to be the radios of a hundred black guys tuned to a hundred different stations.

He'd never had to stay at the police station when they were questioning him about Rory. Cops had been at the hospital and at his parents' and at the factory. They'd come at odd times and asked him the same questions shaped different ways and thought they were so smart.

At first Kevin had rather enjoyed facing them down. It had stopped being a game when they'd influenced other people. Friends who used to call him for tennis doubles or pheasant hunting had become too busy to do anything with Kevin. And they'd begun looking at him oddly.

When Kevin had to play golf alone for the first time in his life, he ceased to be amused by the cops. He hated them. And they hated him.

I was driving, thought Kevin. And I dumped the stuff. I did the trespassing. It's going to be me facing this music of Grey's. And those cops. They've got the music ready. Shit, have they!

His uncle nodded about the police, looking sad and determined, as if being forced to give his daughter away in a mixed marriage. Muscles in his uncle's face twitched. He's serious, thought Kevin.

Grey said, "The radiotelephone."

He can call the cops on that, thought Kevin.

He found himself blocking his uncle, using the rifle for a sort of fence to keep Grey from the phone, saying, "Hey, let's talk about this, Grey."

Grey could not breathe. His body had become rigid, and his lungs were choosing not to inflate. He could feel his diaphragm down there, and it was just resting, uninterested.

The pain that accompanied this was not particularly intense.

The fear was.

A car came around the bend slowly, its headlights displaying them: Grey; Kevin; the truck; the last of the orange guck; the Cadillac half in the road.

A woman was driving. A woman with a halo of dark hair frizzed about a pale face like a carnival doll. Grey tried to call out to her, but nothing in his body was functioning. He was slowly bending over. I'm dying, he thought. What a stupid end to my life.

He tried to draw a breath, wanting to live if for no other reason than to prevent this from being the last chapter.

He didn't want to go out on a sleazy poison crime. "Kevin," he whispered. Kevin had to drive him to the hospital. At least ten miles. He'd never be able to drive alone. He doubted if he could get in the car by himself.

The ambulance service in Holly Oak was run by the police. They'd be better than Kevin. Kevin wouldn't know anything about resuscitation. Grey would not be surprised if Kevin made it a rule not to associate with losers who couldn't breathe anymore. "Police," said Grey, trying to straighten the body that insisted on folding.

When Kevin first began to raise the rifle he'd been toying with, Grey thought he was setting it somewhere so that he could use both arms to support his uncle. Grey watched the angle at which the rifle moved, saw the fingers finding a grip unsuited for setting the object down.

That attack must have been cerebral as well, thought Grey. Affected my peripheral vision or something. Can't seem to figure out what Kevin is doing.

Kevin was turning the muzzle of the gun toward Grey.

The gun was facing him—indeed, it had a little face, a single piggish nostril—and on Kevin's own face was an interested experimental expression.

Shooting me, thought Grey. Does he think I'd turn him in to the police for this? I'm turning myself in. Kevin hasn't done anything except drive my truck. He's my employee, under my orders. Shooting. But you're supposed to take an eye for an eye. This isn't parallel at all, this is— "Stupid," he said to Kevin. I am stupid, the government is stupid, Kevin is supremely stupid. Perhaps life is stupid.

He tried to move, to get behind his car.

He did kill Rory on purpose, Grey thought. The back of Grey's mind was a collage of symphony tickets and poison barrels. The front of it saw Rory tumbling, falling, dying.

Grey even attempted to run, but the slow-motion movement of the gun ceased, and the bullet came out in a blast of blinding white light.

Kevin had plenty of time to think about what he was doing. Like the dieter taking the half gallon of fudge ripple ice cream out of the freezer, he could always put it back before he gave himself a dish. Before he put a spoon in that dish. Before he lifted the spoon to his mouth. Even after the first bite, it was possible to have no more.

But like the dieter, Kevin knew he was not going to stop. It was a most curious, detached feeling, of genuine academic interest. Am I going to shoot my uncle? Why, yes, it appears that I am.

It was not until Grey's blood was pumping into the sand, gurgling like the poisons before it, that it crossed Kevin's mind that prison terms for murder were longer than they could possibly be for liquid littering.

And then he thought: Shit. That woman saw me.

CHAPTER
FIVE

IN THE SOUTH, where partiality to specific religious denominations is very strong, community churches are rare. Holly Oak had one, though, because the visitors represented so many faiths one could not possibly erect enough churches to serve them. (Enough tennis courts and enough golf courses, but those were profitable seven days rather than only one day a week.)

The longleaf pines were a nice asset for Holly Oak Community Church. They carpeted the five acres of church land so that maintenance was confined to the occasional picking up of fallen branches. There were no paths because the needles and the quick-drying sand beneath sufficed. The complete absence of walkways gave the church a boatlike appearance, as if one needed a ramp, not yet pulled out, to get on board. All exterior doors were deeply recessed with no exterior overhang, so that without one's facing the doors squarely, it was difficult to tell where they were.

Hanging on a hook in the second V of the magnolia branches that overhung the main entrance was a key to the sanctuary door. Holly Oak churches were like that. Organ keys were invariably left in the organ bench. Keys to the gold and silver alms basins were in the drawers adjacent to their locked cabinets. Signs on the inside of the church secretaries' closets read: "Key to minister's office under mat." The key in the magnolia was a compromise between the need to prevent vandalism and the belief

that church should always be open for worship. Anyone
who had ever been to the Community Church knew where
the key hung.

Built in the early fifties of antique brick from razed
tobacco warehouses in Sanford, the church reflected its
generation of heavy attendance and popular Sunday school:
It had four connected wings containing sanctuary, classrooms, kitchen/auditorium, and offices over a play school.
The wings had been so well designed that from most angles
there appeared to be only one building with a small ell.
Magnolias and hollies had grown up over the years, and
the church, big as it was, snuggled among them.

Across the road were peach orchards. The acreage to
the west belonged to a stable that boarded trotters over
the winter. Beyond the other boundaries spread the enormous acreage of Holly Oak Country Club, with its six
complete eighteen-hole courses. Sprinkled on the courses
were the Halfway Houses, maintenance buildings, and rain
shelters. Thrusting their little cul-de-sac fingers into the
rough were the residential strips, but the nearest of those
was nearly two miles away from the church.

The woman had been looking right at him. Seen him
the very moment he pulled the trigger. More than likely
seen the blood spurt and the man topple.

Kevin could visualize her perfectly. Dark, massed,
windblown hair—on a summer night this hot, she'd chosen
to drive without the air conditioning on or had none in
her car. Fair skin, large eyes, mouth slightly open. Older.
A white shirt with a necklace that must have been pretty
large for him to register its presence when he'd been occupied with shooting his uncle.

It followed that her recall of him would also be excel-
lent. Kevin, after all, had been caught between her headlights and Grey's.

Kevin jerked the Caddy's keys out of the ignition and
opened the trunk. It was filled with neatly tied newspaper
bundles for the recycling dump. Grabbing the bundles by
the twine, Kevin transferred them to the back seat. He

gripped his uncle's body, folded the knees to make it more compact, and shoved it into into the trunk. Grey had fallen face first into the sand, and the sand had caked on the blood, giving the corpse a gritty texture. Kevin was unable to prevent some of the blood and sand from rubbing off on his shirt.

Get the woman, he thought, slamming the trunk closed.

He leaped back to the truck and got his rifle and the brown paper bag. He had to pick up the ammunition boxes and drop them back in the bag. The slick feel of the clear plastic wrap was intolerable. He did not know if he could wait any longer to rip it off and open the boxes and use the shells.

Can't let her telephone, he thought. Can't let her call anybody.

The Caddy's two left tires were still safely on the pavement. Kevin spurted forward, maneuvered tightly back and forth three times to make the necessary U-turn, and floored the accelerator.

She was noticing the wedding ring on her left hand draped loosely over the curve of the steering wheel. Why am I still wearing that thing anyway? Janney thought. I ought to melt it down and send it to Avery for a suppository.

She passed two men at the side of the road, one of them leaning on a car, the other leaning on a truck. She could not imagine what they were doing there. They looked surreal, as if Janney had caught a glimpse of a huge outdoor movie screen and would never know more of the plot than that single second of action: two men in the woods. There was a peculiar familiarity to the scene, as if she had indeed seen the movie before or as if one of the actors were Avery.

She drove on, confused, bleary.

All the evening's coffee was perking through her body, trying to shake her to the brink of some sort of disaster. I've got to stop drinking coffee, she told herself. Take up something safe. Booze, maybe. I feel alcoholism is something I could really take to.

She was so overwhelmed by the urge to cry that it was difficult to drive. Not, she thought honestly, that I've really been driving up to now. I've just sort of been wheeling along. Bet I haven't looked in my mirror in thirty miles.

As an homage to good driving, Janney looked in her mirror.

A huge, gleaming car was bearing down on her. It glittered on top as if it had a fishpond for a roof. Its headlights were piercing and bulbous, and its engine roared. Pass me, pass me, she told it, and slowed down to annoy the driver into passing. Instead, the car drove so close to her back bumper that she could no longer see its front grille in her mirror. She tried to see the driver, but the lights reflected so that there was nothing but a dark mass on one side of the car.

God, make him pass. I'm almost home. Five miles, maybe. Give me a break, God, let me drive in peace.

On her right a row of mature hollies made prickled lace against a starry sky. Apparently, thought Janney, I'm not an atheist, or I wouldn't be having these talks with God. But I refuse to slip further. Then I'd be one of those religious people I detest so much.

When Ross had been brought home from the VA hospital years ago, the house was filled with religious people. Since Ross refused to have them in his room, it fell to Janney to entertain them. They'd bring casseroles and expect to be chatted with for the next hour. Janney never knew what to say. Yes, Ross is helpless and utterly dependent, aren't the mysterious ways of the Lord intriguing?

And when Donny was killed, the house was wall-to-wall religious people, assuring Janney that since she had no family of her own, her church family would always be there.

And they were. The first week.

*   *   *

Grief was something you were expected to cope with quickly and sensibly. There was something unneighborly about a woman who let her grief lie around in public month after month. The consensus among Janney's religious friends was that if Janney had really been in touch with God, she'd be feeling better by now.

When Avery walked out, though, there seemed to be fewer religious people around than would-be lawyers. Fewer prayers, more advice. All the advice came down to one thing: Put Ross back in the VA hospital. He's too much for you, Janney. This is what paying taxes is for—the Rosses. You aren't obligated to him anyway. He's Avery's son, and Avery is a bastard, so dump Ross.

And Ross in the next room heard this, so when she went in to bring him a tray, he was afraid of her. To Janney it was gruesome in a Hitchcock sort of way that a plain, pleasant middle-aged woman could inspire fear in a young man simply by being able to stand up when he could not. With Ross you always had the upper hand. Literally.

Since his father walked out on them, Ross had become desperate to please Janney. Struggling to do her chores, fix their meals, change his bed himself. Almost invariably he was interrupted by the pain which swept through him like a hurricane through beach cabins. Intractable pain was often constant, but with Ross it came in jolts, and unfortunately a jolt was apt to hit when he was drying a glass, which would then slip from his fingers and splinter on the tile, meaning one more job for Janney. And the house had not been built for someone in a wheelchair. Even when he felt fine, Ross could not reach the clean sheets in the linen closet or the glasses in the sink. She had to do so much preparation in order to allow Ross to help that it only served to irritate her. And therefore, when she too needed to talk, share, hug, complain, weep, he almost cringed in her presence. The times when he was the Ross he'd been before the accident—calm, funny, relaxed—were rare and cherished.

Accident. That was how people liked to refer to it. Janney felt there was something inherently nonaccidental

about war injuries. But religious people loved euphe-
misms.

And speaking of accidents, she thought, I am about to
have one. What is the matter with that drunk behind me?
He's trying to neck with my license plate.

Of all her trials, surely driving was the worst. She was
neither a good nor a happy driver. She made a fine pas-
senger. And for the rest of our lives, I'm Ross's driver, she
thought. How totally miserable for us both.

Oh, Lord, I'm sick of a sense of duty.

Bet there was a psalmist who sang that to you, too, only
some fundamentalist deleted it three thousand years ago.

It was hard to see the idiot car behind her through the
mist of tears that blocked her vision. I need to cry, Janney
thought. A long, long cry, with nobody around, so I can
really lean into the sobs and let them rack me. Rack. Such
a good word. Fraught with medieval torture instruments.

For a brief moment her lights illuminated the tiny old
burying ground behind the Community Church. A lot of
people died in Holly Oak, having, after all, come there to
do so, but the town kept most of its cemeteries discreetly
hidden. Donny wasn't buried there. He was in Boston beside her parents.

The more slowly she drove, hoping to shake the fool
behind her, the more a thick honeysuckle and magnolia
perfume drifted through the hot summer air and into the
car with her. It was like having Donny still in his car seat,
eating his apples.

He'd been a confirmed apple freak. When she'd finally
managed to go into his room after the funeral, the plaid
walls and red rug seemed to emanate the cidery odor that
Donny had always carried around with him. She'd found
a picture book in which her son had used an apple core
for a bookmark. The hardest thing Janney ever did was
throw away that apple, its little bits of browned flesh pre-
serving the spot where Donny's crooked teeth had sunk.

The next day Avery left.

She had almost become religious then. She and Ross
even read psalms aloud to each other. But, as Ross pointed

out, for every psalmist singing a new song unto the Lord, there were scores of poor souls so hideously afflicted they made Job's life sound like fun. None of the psalms had any handy historical footnotes to say, Oh, yes, the Lord took pity about five years later, and everyone lived happily ever after.

Truly I am on the verge of falling, said afflicted psalmist number thirty-eight, and my pain is always with me.

Janney did not know to which of them it applied more: herself or Ross.

The breath that filled her lungs shivered its way in, catching on the corners in her throat, choking her.

Oh, God.

She could not tolerate the glaring, hateful headlights that were trespassing on her. If the jerk wouldn't pass her, then she'd leave the road.

Janney swerved abruptly and almost without slowing skidded over the pine needles into the driveway of the Holly Oak Community Church.

The night was endless, like all nights for Ross.

You're not trying, Ross, his father used to say to him. If you'd just put your mind to it, you could rise above this pain of yours. Pretend you're an airplane pilot. Fly above it.

Dad, he'd say, desperate with frustration, I can't even get into the plane, let alone fly it.

Just try, Ross! You're not trying!

Sometimes Ross felt they all would do better if he were a real prisoner, with shackles and chains. Then Avery would be unable to claim that Ross could jump up if he only had the right attitude.

Avery'd been immensely proud of Donny. The way, once, he'd been proud of Ross.

Donny was a born entrepreneur, and Avery reveled in his son's enterprises. One of Donny's moneymaking schemes involved the strategic placement of empty Jell-O boxes around the property. Taped to these were clever signs meant to entice the unwary passerby. "Drop your money in here," Ross had printed for his brother.

That day Ross had been on the porch in his wheelchair, letting the hot sun cook out some of the pain, when Donny came back from checking his boxes for money. "Getting rich?" said Ross.

"No," said Donny sadly. "Hey, Ross?" Instantly brightening. "On 'Captain Kangaroo' this morning they read people's palms. Can I read your palm for you?"

"No," said Ross, who did not like to think about the future.

"Then I'll read your knuckles."

But Ross hadn't felt like laughing or cooperating, and Donny took off through the yard, being a horse. Whinnying, and then being a car, yelling, "Vroom, vroom, vroom!" Donny changed gears to "Yom! Yom! Yom!" and for veracity's sake headed into the road.

Both Ross and Janney saw what was coming, and yelled, and Janney ran, while all Ross could do was tighten his fingers around the rim of his wheelchair, but the car was going too fast, and Donny never saw it.

Ross often looked at his left hand, the one whose palm Donny had wanted to read, and wondered if his little brother would be alive if he'd opened his fist.

The answer was always yes.

He did not know how Janney could bear to have him around, let alone care for him. At least she'd taken down all of Donny's yard crosses. He wondered if she had stripped Donny's bedroom. Ross had never been in Donny's room. Ross had never even been upstairs. Avery had turned the dining room and back pantry into a suite for Ross, with exit ramps from both the living room and the kitchen out to a gently sloping blacktopped path which led to the golf cart track below.

He could understand Avery's leaving. He'd gladly have left himself. But for Ross there was no going anywhere except very possibly to the veterans hospital.

It wasn't so bad before, he told himself. Lots of people to talk to. Volunteers to push me around. Arts and crafts whether I want them or not. Little groups of this and that, analyzing each other's hang-ups.

No privacy, no peace, no family, no exit.

Oh, Janney, come home, he thought. God, I'm so lonely.

He looked at the clock again. She was very late.

Churches meant organs to Janney, not rest.

Yet when her headlights glittered against the old distorted glass of the only two visible windows, she had an almost primitive sense that the church would truly be a sanctuary.

Let myself in with the key, she thought. Go into the bride's room and weep. Or play the organ. Haven't played a decent organ in two years. It would be comforting to play their Casavant.

The idea startled her. After all, where was it written that she had to drive straight home after work?

She turned so fast she almost lost control on the slippery needles and narrowly missed the trunk of an old longleaf pine.

As the headlights behind her stayed on Deep River Road, Janney began thinking about what to play. Something splashy? Something big and blazing that would fill her up with sound instead of depression? That would have to be French. Vierne? Widor? Franck?

The big shiny car's brakes screamed viciously on the blacktop.

For Janney the shriek of brakes was a dead child.

She had her left hand on the interior door handle and her right turning off the Pinto engine. Her hands leaped in shock at the sound of the brakes. She seemed to be propelled out of her own car, as if horror were shoveling her off the seat, thrusting her into the churchyard. Donny, Donny! she thought, and the same adrenaline that had sent her racing desperately after him surged through her.

Some female instinct made her lift up her purse as she went, but she had no driver's instinct to take the car keys as well.

The big car, which had passed the church drive by another car's length, reversed noisily and turned into the drive after her.

The car that had hit Donny had been large. Oh, God, so large. So many heavy wheels, so much crunching metal.

She whirled and ran for the safety of the church.

The big car stopped, its door opened, and as she lifted the key from the magnolia tree, a man got out.

His open front door turned on the interior light of his car, and in the instant before he slammed the door she could see him perfectly. He was young. Wearing a short-sleeved knit shirt that was too tight, girdling his muscles in a way that preteen girls probably loved. Cutoff jeans displaying the body of a man who isn't kidding when he says he's going to run a few miles. He seemed posed for a film on campus jocks, or an advertisement for tennis rackets, with his legs spread in a confident V.

For me a V is a diminuendo, she thought; for him it's victory.

He reached back into the car for a long, thin rod. When a Holly Oak man held something like that, it was generally a golf club. But golf clubs came in sets and were found near golf courses. You might play tennis or softball by night lights, but not golf.

And nobody ever held a golf club like that.

There was something equally sinister and comical about the stance, beside a dogwood, in front of a country church.

A gun, thought Janney Fraser. It's *a gun*.

CHAPTER
SIX

KEVIN CLARY was a vandal.

It was a secret pleasure. In all his reading of letters to the editors of men's magazines, he had never come across anyone else who shared his feelings. Other men seemed to revel in curious sexual endeavors that Kevin loved reading about but never wanted to emulate.

He had begun small, as small boys do. The first thing Kevin ever did was knock down a neighbor's mailbox. There was a thick, hot joy in hearing the family complain to his parents about what the world was coming to. About how the post was bent and they had to buy a new one and the red mail signal was broken off and they couldn't find a replacement.

I did that, thought Kevin, proudly.

He found himself opening gates to let horses out of fenced pastures onto busy roads. Jerking antennas off hoods, breaking pulleys on flagpoles, and shooting out windows in the old vacated black elementary schools.

A church, thought Kevin.

He could not imagine why he had never vandalized a church.

The woman bounded from her car, leaping and passing like a squirrel caught in the middle of the road. He did not move, needing to watch her. The bullet would move for him.

She'd sure as hell seen him. He wondered what had

attracted her to the church as a place to go. It was obviously empty, locked, and isolated.

Telephone, he thought. She's probably even got the license of Grey's car to tell the cops. Though with a car like that, who needs to have a license?

There was no way to saunter home and pretend somebody else had killed Grey Randallman, not when Aunt Catherine and the whole symphony board probably knew Grey had gone to meet Kevin somewhere. He was going to have to run. The important thing was to give himself as much running time as possible, and that meant the woman could not be allowed to get to her church telephone.

His mind seemed to be working with incredible stupendous rapidity, selecting moves and options like an automatic chess game.

Leave Grey's car here, he thought. A classic like that, anybody'd recognize it anywhere. Run across the golf course to the Yamaha repair shop and take a motorcycle. Be out of the state by dawn.

Like the TV show, he thought. Like "The Fugitive."

He saw himself: tall, slim, good-looking, his face creased with tough determination that would lead him through chase, adventure, and romance.

The woman moved away from the protective branches of her chosen tree and completely exposed herself in his headlights. Against the soft red brick of the church wall he could see that she was older than he had first thought. Practically his mother's age.

He lifted the rifle, sighted—and she vanished. Kevin blinked. It was as if the building had absorbed her.

Something burst in Kevin. It was hot and thick, like having too much blood. He found himself breathing faster, feeling both anger and excitement, and he thought exultantly: I've got to get her. Get her!

At first Janney thought she would never be able to close the door after her. It had an automatic cushioning device to keep it from slamming, and it would not pull shut. It drifted. She could hear the man's feet on the pine needles.

It hadn't rained in so long that the needles were crunchy and dry, like breakfast cereal.

Her frantic pulling was having no effect on the huge, thick door at all. It would close in its own good time. He'll walk right in, she thought, as if I'm being courteous and holding it open for him.

Gently, slowly the door clicked shut and locked itself. Janney backed away from it. Under her feet the texture changed from vestibule carpet to the antique brick of the sanctuary. She leaned against the carved threshold and tried to breathe, but her chest had turned to cement.

The man had looked familiar. Robin? She had substituted for Robin often. She knew the organ and church well. Robin belonged to the fling-yourself-all-over-the-keyboard-and-toss-your-head-in-ecstasy school of performance. Janney never saw Robin play without wanting to rope his shoulders down.

It's not Robin out there, she thought, trying to tell herself it was not a gun either. Robin never practiced, and anyhow, he lived in Winston-Salem and drove down only for Sunday services, choir rehearsal, and lucrative weddings.

She waited, praying the man would call to her. Would say, "Janney, it's me, what are you afraid of?"

Instead, she saw the man's head, which was all that reached high enough to show, in the windows, bobbing down the length of the church, looking for the entrance.

So it was not the minister, who would probably recognize the way in, although knowing Dr. Royalls, she was not entirely sure of this, and it wasn't a local policeman, who would surely have checked the church enough to know where the doors were. Besides policemen in Holly Oak drove pale blue Volkswagens with roof lights so large they resembled fruit baskets on small tables.

She became aware that her palm was hurting, and she saw that she had been holding the door key so tightly it had made dents in her hand.

The man found the door. Janney gagged. The knob moved a quarter inch to the left and stopped, and then a quarter inch to the right and stopped. There was a pause. The man shook the door handle hard.

She could not seem to run. It seemed far more intelligent to stay there, keeping track of him, than to flee down the dark corridors toward the telephone, through corridors that seemed a lot darker and a lot more threatening than they ever had before.

The lights of his car bathed half the church in a shadowy light. The Casavant organ was semiexposed, and the visible pipes gleamed in a geometric cascade from their beautifully grained wind chests. The dimness gave the church a warm, waiting feel, as if God really had planned to attend and would be there momentarily.

The man left the door, and she watched his head when it appeared in the sanctuary window. The head acquired shoulders and a body and then legs, which carried it back to its car.

Oh, thank God, he was leaving.

Janney was always surprised that relief was a weakening sensation while fear was strengthening. You would think it would be the reverse: that when things were okay, you could saunter off, and when things were bad, your knees would buckle. Instead, her knees were giving way now that the man was leaving.

She tottered into the church and sat on the organ bench, which was at the rear of the church, directly opposite the distant altar. She detested playing with her back to the congregation. Using mirrors during a service made the whole thing somewhat like driving a car.

The man turned off his car headlights. In the darkness Janney felt an unexpected dose of safety.

The church smelled of peace and grape juice, old coats and dust.

Bach, she thought. As long as I'm here, I may as well play. And it has to be Bach. After all, *eleven* of his children died before he did. Maybe I can absorb some of his faith.

She swiveled on the bench and lifted off the console lid. It was Plexiglas with teak handles and looked to Janney like something totally unrelated to the organ, as if it had fallen off a passing yacht. She was bending down to set it on the floor when she realized that the motor of the big, hulking car had not started up again.

Her scalp crawled. He isn't gone, she thought. He pretended to go. Oh, my God, why would he do *that?* What's he—

The door in the sacristy opened.

She did not think she had ever heard a sound as horrid as that door creaking open. Her eyes burned with tears of fear, and her heart iced over.

How churchy, she thought lucidly. How like a church to lock the front door and forget about the others.

The sacristy was a small room beside the choir loft and altar, thirty pews distant. To come into the sanctuary with her, the man would have to walk ten feet or so to open another door. To get into the vestibule, out of his sight, and start her run for the offices, Janney would have to cross at least thirty exposed feet.

She dropped the lid, forgetting about the brick on which it would crash. Next to the console was an access door to the pipe room, fronted with false pipes so it would blend into the façade. She pushed the swinging door and leaned on it to stop the creaking and wondered if he had come out of the sacristy in time to see her.

In the dark he would never notice the access door.

In the light he probably would.

It's not a crazy man with a gun, Janney told herself.

Her heart hurt. Her rib cage seemed to have shrunk.

It's probably a concerned parishioner, she thought. Figures he needs a gun to stop the thief bent on making off with the gold offertory plates. All I have to do is say, "Yoohoo, it's me, crazy old Janney Fraser. You know how we musicians get these whims in the wee hours."

But a concerned parishioner would not have been following her so closely, braking so violently.

Janney's hands were dripping wet. They were cold, too. The cold moved in back of her eyes, freezing her thoughts.

And how do I get out of here? she thought hysterically. If he marches up and shoves this door in, then what? She had to see what was happening. She could not bear her position against the little hinged door, huddling, God knew what was happening out there.

She wondered if God did know.

The man was walking. Walking toward her, down the central aisle, directly toward the organ. She found herself gripping a nearby pipe for support, and it merely lifted up in her hand out of its hole, so that she had to keep it too absolutely motionless, lest it clink against all the others in its rank.

The footsteps came right up to the organ.

Janney's chest inflated about as well as a piece of wood. She tried to remember her voice lessons decades ago, about the diaphragm and lung control.

Her cheek was pressed against the scratchy particle board of the back of the door. She could see nothing. Pipe rooms were intended for the most efficient placement of thousands of pipes in dozens of rows at multiple levels in the least possible space. They were not—

There was the definite, precise sound of a zipper zipping.

Exposing himself to the organ console? she thought.

Then a shuffling noise, papery, jangly.

My purse, she thought, he's opening my purse, and relief made her knees buckle again, but if she moved, she would strike the metal pipes and he would find her.

Go, rob me of my Susan B. Anthony dollar, she thought. Take the pennies, too, and the used-up lipstick and the credit cards that expired last year.

Her purse had four tiny metal feet. She knew the sound when he set it back on the bench. If I can just stand here and be absolutely silent, I'll be okay. That's the operative thing, keeping silent. If he knew I was in here, he'd have come in after me by now.

The man took a breath through his nose, a sort of thoughtful, backwards sigh. The shoes moved away from the organ.

She remembered the time last year when Ross was hospitalized with pneumonia and she was home alone and she called the police because she kept hearing someone walking around. The police were there impressively fast, and right away they found the sneakers thudding around and around in the dryer. They hadn't laughed at her. They'd been horribly, gently, depressingly kind. She'd felt retarded.

I am retarded, she thought. I actually decided to go alone into a deserted church in the middle of the night to play Bach.

There was a loud, vicious, ripping sound.

Janney's head yanked back as if her hair had been pulled. She lowered her chin with her fingers and tried to calm herself. The sound was like that of old sheets being shredded into rags, but larger, longer, more destructive. The ripping seemed to eat at her skin.

She *had* to see what was happening. The blindness of her position was intolerable. She felt around, fingers exploring the wooden edges that contained pipes, looking for a ledge that would be wide enough and empty enough to be the catwalk the organ tuner used. She found it, knee high. Balancing her fingertips on the doorjamb, she climbed carefully to the unseen little shelf. Turning herself, trying to slim her body so it wouldn't catch on any pipes, she faced out through the acoustical cloth that covered the chamber and looked into the moonlit church.

He was tearing the flags. The American flag, the state flag, and now a beautiful ecclesiastical banner. She could not see his face, only the work of his hands. Great, strong hands, to rip through the wide hems and thick material.

He's crazy, thought Janney.

The *z* in the word seemed to rip along with the flags. *Crazy*.

A muscle in her thigh began to convulse. She pressed her palm against the muscle to stop it, but this only made her hand twitch, too.

God, you remember that time of trouble I keep mentioning to you? This is it. Don't be like Avery and run out on me. Be here when I need you.

The man stopped tearing the banner, walked over to the pulpit, and turned on the lights.

There was no way of knowing whether or not he could see her silhouette. Whether she was merely another pipe-like vertical shadow...or an obvious female outline.

Having the lights on had one advantage: They cast a bit of shadowy light into the pipe room and showed her, twelve feet distant, the other entrance to the chamber. She had forgotten it. It opened into the cloakroom of the vestibule.

The crazy man walked directly toward her for the second time. No, Janney told herself, it's only that the aisle leads to the organ. He has not seen me. Probably knows nothing about organs. Maybe he doesn't even know what pipes are or that they require a room for themselves. Probably thinks the entire organ is displayed on the wall in front of him.

With a rifle in one hand and a long red shred of flag in the other, the man nevertheless managed to look normal and content with life, as if he were propman for a stage play and this were all a game. He began smiling. The smile grew larger and larger until Janney thought it would burst. When he dropped the cloth and put one hand to his mouth, she thought he was going to rip his mouth the way he had the flags.

Do I know him in the sense that I know fear, and he is fear? thought Janney. She struggled with her faint recognition of the man. He could not have anything to do with her job at the mall; those headlights had not been behind her all that way. He was new. He had just appeared. Soon after she'd seen those two men by the road, the ones standing so oddly at the sides of their vehicles, he was—one of *them,* she thought, utterly confused. But what—

"Hello, Laura," said the man in a low, sexy voice. He grinned right at her and raised the rifle with a terrible swiftness. Laura? she thought. *Laura?*

Janney leaped forward, praying she wouldn't impale herself on the tiny, pencil-sharp row of reeds, and landed on the small square of open floor where the opposite door's swing space was. I need a weapon, too, she thought.

The man's feet smashed on the brick, coming after her.

Janney reached for a diapason that looked as if it would be in battle what it was in music—a good solid beginning—and flung open the door to the cloakroom just as the hinges of the other swung inward behind her.

I am poured out like water, said the psalmist. All my bones are out of joint, and my heart within my breast is like melting wax.

Janney raced down the steps to the hall that led to the office wing, past opened doors gaping down black caverns of stairwells. Come on, God, "yea, though I walk through the valley" and so forth, she thought.

Someone had left a wooden classroom chair in the middle of the hall. Janney ran into it full speed and was flung on her face. She caught herself with both hands, bending her wrists backward. Half sobbing, dropping the organ pipe, she staggered to her feet and headed for the dusty rose Exit sign glowing beyond her. The office was around the corner.

Telephone, let me remember how to dial, don't let me panic that much.

Behind her was a grunt. Not an oomph as if the wind had been knocked out when he located the same wooden chair, but a grunt of animal satisfaction. Like a hog, rooting, chasing, and ripping.

Janney had a friend who kept hogs. Are they dangerous? said Janney, appalled at how large they were. No, said her friend reflectively. As long as you don't get between the hog and the feed.

Janney grabbed the office door and turned the knob.

It was locked.

Oh, God, she thought.

The crazy man's footsteps turned into the corridor where she stood.

CHAPTER
SEVEN

FOR ONE MOMENT Kevin felt real fear. He had absolutely no idea what he was looking at. Hundreds of thrusting objects blocked his path. Thick, thin, round, square, inches high, twenty feet high, wooden, metal. A dated science-fiction view of another planet's housing. In a church, where everything should be ordinary, contemptible.

He backed out, his heart jerking painfully in his chest. It humiliated him that he didn't know what the room was.

But through the opened door from which she'd fled, he could see into the cloakroom and, beyond that, the vestibule, conveniently lit up from when he'd thrown all the other switches. Kevin turned off the sanctuary lights so passersby wouldn't see the church was occupied and ran after her.

There was only one corridor, so she'd had no choice. He crouched to listen. He could actually hear her running, a faint series of puffs on the carpet. Headed for a phone, he thought. That's going to be in an office.

He could not believe how well he could hear her. The church had superb acoustics, even out here in the hall.

It isn't the church, Kevin thought, it's me. If I could feel this way all the time, I could win everything.

Away from the rippled windowpanes where the moonlight drizzled in it was dark as pitch. He stumbled, not expecting the hall to have stairs. Every few yards he paused to listen and then, half crouching, half running, rushed after the woman.

The memory of the ripping was in his hands, as if his skin and his nails and his muscles had instant recall. It was infinitely more pleasurable to destroy something symbolic than any ordinary object. He shivered, feeling the flags again, seeing the fabric bunch and fight him and resist—and tear. A tic began in his cheek.

At a turn in the corridor Kevin hesitated. She could have gone anywhere. They'd now moved into the ell of the church that was invisible from the street, and he could turn the lights on if he chose.

But it was like sex. Better in the dark.

He carried the rifle in front of him, commando style. His whole body seemed to blaze with panting excitement. What a night! First a deer. Then his uncle. And now a *woman*, to be tracked and hunted down like—

He distinguished a clicking sound.

A gun? Kevin thought, and he was actually angry. It was not fair for her to be armed. Abruptly he wanted the lights on after all. He began feeling the walls for switches, his hands whispering over the smooth plaster. The wall on the right side of the corridor seemed to be blank. He tried the left. Nothing. A few steps toward the clicks into an utterly black hall, and he found the switch plates about six feet past the turn.

The faint noises stopped. He could hear her breathing. He raised the rifle with his left hand, getting it at just the right angle so his right hand could turn on the lights and go immediately to the trigger. But the lights made him blink, and she was on the opposite side of the corridor from where he'd expected her to be, and as he made the adjustments, she moved quicker than a rabbit, vanishing into a hole next to her before he even had his right hand solidly on the rifle.

He did not so much as swear. He was not even aware of himself thinking, or choosing, because the necessity to move faster than Laura didn't give him time.

Stairs. She was clattering down them. There was no

way he could shoot blindly into such a confined area. It took Kevin several precious seconds to find the stairwell light switch, which wasn't directly at the head of the steps but several feet before them, right by the office door, the vanilla-colored plate blending invisibly with the vanilla-painted walls.

His rage was expanding. It included time, which he was wasting, and the electrician, whose pattern he had not yet figured out, and the church itself, which was too big. His cheek jerked, and it set off a responsive chord in his trigger finger, so that the finger truly itched, like poison ivy, wanting to tug.

He leaped down the metal steps after her. The lights, infuriatingly, lit just one end of the next hall, so he caught only a shadowy sense of movement at the far end where she disappeared and wasted more time finding the next switch, getting to the next turn.

He could not understand the extent of the buildings. What was all this space *for?*

The woman kept running. If she went to ground in one of these rooms, it would be hell to smoke her out. But as long as she was so panicky, spurting in front of him like water from a hose, he'd get her.

They made a full circuit, ending up near the offices again and back down the stairs to the basement corridor. Since he had not turned any of the lights off and since he was only a dozen or so yards behind her, he knew for sure she hadn't managed to get out of the lower hall. She'd gone into one of the little rooms. Kevin stopped short at the bottom of the stairs, controlling his own panting, listening for Laura's.

Nothing.

After extending a hand inside the first door, he scrabbled along the wall to find the lights. Without leaving the doorway, keeping one eye on the hall and that escape route, he examined the room he'd lit up. It was a class for very small children. Tiny wooden chairs. A feltboard display of "Our Families" and "Our Town." On the right wall were two more doors. Storage closets maybe? Connecting doors to other classrooms? Bathrooms?

If he went in to look, he'd be unable to watch the hall, and certainly her plan would be to sneak out while he was occupied with the search. Kevin left the closets for the moment and went to the door of the next room. It was almost closed, and when he gave it a gentle push, it creaked and resisted him. He pushed it slowly until it banged against the wall. She wasn't standing behind it anyway. He looked into the dark room.

The room winked back at him, eyes glittering, staring, watching him. Kevin's cheek jerked. He thought of the room with its thrusting objects and its vaguely satanic, meaningless atmosphere, and it seemed to him the classroom was filled with cats, evil black cats, staring at him, and he was prickling with nervous sweat when he found the light switch and turned it and there were the glass eyes of puppets. Dozens of orange- and green-haired purple-nosed puppets.

What kind of church was this anyway?

This room, too, had doors. And cabinets. A desk with hidden knee space. A movable puppet stage behind which two or three adults could huddle.

But what Laura would want was not so much a hiding place as a telephone.

He was having difficulty thinking. For the first time in his life Kevin seemed to have too much energy. I'm high, he thought dizzily, although he had never taken any kind of drug; he was far too much of a fitness addict to do that to his body.

He checked the third classroom, but it was entirely bare. Not even one chair. It, too, had extra doors.

His breath was coming faster and faster, and he could no longer keep it quiet enough so Laura could not hear him. Like the puppets, he seemed to have dozens of eyes, looking everywhere, and as many ears, listening for everything.

But there was nothing to see, nothing to hear.

The last door in the hall was an exit, although there

was no neon sign to say so. Small letters bought at the hardware store and pasted on said "EXIT." Christ! She'd been out and gone ten minutes!

Kevin shoved down on the spring handle of the door, so angry he wanted to tear it off, bend the door, feeling the rage right down to his teeth, so that he could have bitten the door in his rage—and it was locked.

An exit door. Locked from the inside.

Have to speak to the fire marshal about this, Kevin thought, and he grinned. The tic in his cheek ceased. He went back to start checking the closets.

They'd brought Ross home from the VA hospital after fourteen months. There'd been six men in his ward, six in the next, and the next, and the next. Legless, armless, eyeless, sometimes mindless, and, more often than not, visitorless.

About the only suffering Ross did not endure was nightmares of Vietnam; he'd been there only two days when he was hurt. If it had been just paralysis, he could have taken up a fairly normal adulthood, even gone on to basketball and golf; there were wheelchair clubs. But there was also a severe dizziness from the head injuries that kept him prostrate on his bad days, and headaches so bad it was like having something in there chewing on his bones.

When Avery and Janney got him home, Ross spent nearly a year just lying there on the bed, watching a patch of sunlight move slowly across the red and blue quilt Janney had made for him out of bandannas. He could have tolerated the female attention more if she had been his real mother, whose obligations of blood and birth would be unquestioned, but Janney was merely his father's new wife. She'd met and married Avery when Ross was in the army. She had not expected an invalid adult male to be part of the package. She owed Ross nothing.

For years he disliked her kindness more than he appreciated it.

Yet in the end it was Janney, not his father who became Ross's only ally.

Be strong! Avery liked to cry, like some prophet of yore. Forget the vertigo! Ride over the headaches! The only handicap is in your mind!

He'd tried. But his father was wrong: The handicaps were in his body.

Over and over Peter used to say to him, So life is different. There's nothing you can do. Work with what you've got.

And what he had was an hour or two a day at most when he felt good, or what passed for good in his worthless body, and that time in minute-long shifts. And then Ross didn't want to do anything except revel in the lack of pain.

Of all the streams of young men and old women who'd come to help after Peter, not one had been a friend, or reliable, or willing to continue for long. The only memorable aide was an old country woman who didn't stay because, as she said, she didn't like to have truck with a patient who wasn't a bona fide southerner.

Bonified. It sounded as if it referred to skeletal strength.

She's right, said Avery grimly, when the old woman quit. Ross isn't bonified.

Ross thought of it every day. Every goddamned day. Ross isn't bonified.

Without me on her shoulder, he thought, Janney'd be okay. Probably go back to Boston and her friends there and do just fine.

He pictured Janney doing just fine.

Since it was the only decision he'd ever be able to make, Ross wanted to choose to go back, not be sent, to the VA hospital. He wanted to arrange for the ambulance himself, not have Janney courteously announce it. It would be, he thought, a bona fide gesture. Absolve him of some of the guilt of lying around.

Except that it would not be a gesture. It would be for good.

The only times he would see anyone but staff or patients would be when Janney felt like visiting, and how often would that be? Knowing the memories the sight of

Ross would stir? His father would never come. His father would never even know.

Ross loathed the word *visitor*. Even isolated as he was, he'd come to know the Holly Oak use of the word. *Visitor* meant golf and tennis and muscles that responded when you told them to.

It would be a gift, he told himself. About the only gift I ever could give Janney.

He jeered at himself. Think I can retrieve the old macho image, don't I? he thought. Think I can still be the traditional muscle-bound breadwinner and protect the little woman from harm. Prove that chivalry is not yet dead by walking out of her life. Or being wheeled out.

Another headache began. Ross's headaches overlapped, so that as the pain of one receded, the next moved in. Like a slow surf.

And no low tide. Ever.

Janney lay behind the puppets. Her chest ached from the throbbing of her heart. Her ribs weren't used to so much pounding. She was trapped. He was guarding the two exits from the corridor up to the next level, and the exit door she'd counted on was locked. *Laura.* He'd called her Laura. But then who could he be? Someone from the very distant past? But if that were so, how could he be the man by the side of the road? And why would *anyone* want to come after her? After seven-pounds-overweight forty-year-old Janney?

How interesting that when I describe myself, I always put my seven pounds first. I must have a very low self-image. Ross and I should go to assertiveness training courses.

That sort of thing probably wasn't offered in Holly Oak. People who lived there seemed to be assertive enough for two. And Ross and I, Janney thought, we aren't assertive enough for one.

Laura. She had not been called Laura since the first day of kindergarten, when there were four Lauras in her class and they decided to call her by her last name, Janney.

The man tried the last classroom door. His heavy shoes turned on the carpet with a slight squeak, and inadvertently his lips formed the same faint meditative whistle he'd made in church.

He had not examined any of the rooms. That would have to come next. But he'd be tricky. He'd want her to think he was deep in a closet next door while really he was ready with that gun in the hall.

A gun.

It was beyond credence. You didn't bring your gun to church and go after the organist.

She had chosen a ridiculous spot to hide: lying on her side under a row of puppets. She was utterly helpless. She could not get up easily and almost certainly could not get up silently. He had only to walk in and scrutinize the room more carefully, and he'd probably see her feet or hair.

On the other hand, he would be looking in the logical hiding spots first: closets, cabinets, and stage.

She might still have a chance.

And what if she didn't?

What would happen to Ross if she were not there? It was not true that an individual is always dispensable. "Let us replace your man," said the personnel slogans, as if one man were just like the next. Lies. Avery-type lies. Ross had no one to replace Janney.

It was curious how much she despised Avery now. All the things fine and good in Avery were permanently tarnished by his leaving. It would not surprise her if when she took the wedding ring to a gold and silver exchange (they were proliferating like fast-food restaurants), it turned out to be mere yellow-dyed metal.

The man and his shoes were heavy. His walk thumped. He was trying to walk softly, but the floor vibrated when his weight came down and gave him away.

And from the next classroom came a noise so horrible and rasping she thought something must be eating the man, chewing him up. She clutched one of the puppets, hugging it to her, a toddler with her precious dolly. The grip of her muscles around the puppet somehow kept her from crying out.

The noise came again, and a third time, and by then it was not so terrifying and she could actually identify it.

He was ripping the doors off the storage cabinets.

The furry hair of the puppets crawled on her neck. Or was it her own hair crawling on the puppets?

The crazy man crossed the hall to the room opposite hers, and she could see him now through the door. When he turned on the light, she saw it was an arts and crafts room. Decorating the near wall were a half dozen crosses made of twigs laboriously tied together by small Sunday school hands. With his left hand the man snapped them, rubbing his fingers together until the crosses were a grit that fell messily to the floor. His right hand gently swung the rifle.

Insane, thought Janney. Dear God, I'm trapped in a church basement with a rifle-carrying lunatic.

The man moved out of her range of vision, and she knew there would be cabinets in that room, too, full of finger paints and construction paper, and she got her muscles ready. The minute the ripping began, she was up and running, throwing puppets aside like rain off an umbrella. She leaped up the stairs, through the lighted corridors that illuminated her like a painted target, back to the vestibule door. She could feel the man behind her as much as hear him. Thudding footsteps shook the church as if it were built of toothpicks instead of bricks.

There was some sort of dreadful bottled anger in the man that was even more terrifying than the rifle. The rifle, after all, was predictable. It would spit bullets at her.

She did not know, could not understand, what the man would do. To Laura.

She was out the door. No point in going to the cars or the road. She could never get her car started, turned around, and past his car before he emerged from the church.

Get into the trees, she thought, she who was normally afraid of the dark and isolated herself from it with walls, curtains, and shades. But in the trees there could be no lights to expose protruding feet. She rushed into the dark as if it were something safe and soft and cuddly.

Ducking under the holly trees, ignoring the painful scrape on her cheek, she churned over the too-yielding pine needles toward the thickets that lined the left side of the church property.

Between her and the dark clotted safety of the shrubbery was a barbed-wire fence.

"Mrs. Randallman?" said the police officer. "We drove up to the mill, like you asked, but the parking lot fence is locked, the factory entrance is locked, and there are no cars around and no lights on."

"Oh," said Catherine. She was staring at her watch. She'd been watching each minute making its slow circular pass until ninety of them had gone by and still Grey was not home.

"No accident reports, and nobody's come to the emergency room that could be Mr. Randallman. They know him there, anyway, you know, from his volunteer work with the bloodmobile."

"Oh," said Catherine. The palms of her hands prickled with damp and slid around the telephone. Why was she not relieved by this? Why did it all suddenly seem worse? "What shall I do now?" she asked him. Because I have no explanation, she thought. Because a car accident was a safer explanation than Kevin laughing.

"If I were you, ma'am, I'd go back to bed. He'll call or get home shortly, I'm sure."

"Isn't there something else you can do?"

"Well, we'll kind of keep an eye out, ma'am."

She had not yet mentioned Kevin's name. Or his phone call. Just said Grey was late. "But it's after one o'clock in the morning. Grey isn't home. He's always home."

Up until now she had liked Bob Shearing. Now his voice took on a bored, superior, masculine coloration that made her jaws tighten. There was, he said, with a deep courtesy, always a first time, and this must be it. "Adults aren't considered missing persons until twenty-four hours have

passed, Mrs. Randallman. Whatever he had planned after
the symphony board meeting must just be taking longer
than he thought. Try not to worry about it."

"Twenty-four hours!" she cried. "But what if something
dreadful has happened? He could—well, I don't know what
he could, but twenty-four hours is a long time."

"Do you have reason to suspect foul play?" said Shearing, with the same deep courtesy that for some reason was
infuriating.

Foul play, she thought, and the air conditioning that
had not been cool enough earlier descended on her skin
like ice. Bob Shearing knew Kevin from that—that Rory
thing. If she said Kevin had been the one whose errand
had taken Grey away from the symphony board, Shearing
would draw the wrong conclusions. He would think—would
think—Catherine swallowed against what the police might
think. "No," she said, "of course not. But something must
have happened!"

He said maybe if she got off the phone, Grey could call
her up and tell her what the problem was.

Catherine obeyed.

Now there were three things to watch: the driveway,
the minute hand, and the telephone. I must call him back,
she thought. Admit what I'm thinking about Kevin. But
my in-laws would never forgive me. They'd never speak
to me again. Even Grey might never speak—

She closed her mind, rigidly, and focused on her three
objects.

CHAPTER
EIGHT

JANNEY had always considered Christianity an exclusionary sort of religion, but she would not have said its adherents went to such lengths as to protect themselves with barbed wire.

She'd torn her clothes but not her flesh. Janney ripped her blouse free and fled the other way. She'd lost her chance to slip into the woods and lie low until the man gave up. Now she was like a squirrel in the middle of the road, rushing back and forth while the crushing tire closed in.

The people on the far side didn't need barbed wire. They had bamboo.

Bamboo seemed like a good idea when you saw a few sticks of it: slim, elegant, tropical. But each year the bamboo ate up more ground, like a Soviet army with no intention of ever giving up, until it formed an impenetrable forest of tens of thousands of rigid rods only an inch or two apart.

Bamboo to the right of her, barbed wire to the left of her. It sounded like "The Charge of the Light Brigade." Onward, onward, into the jaws of—

God, this is too much, Janney said. She could hear the man coming out of the church, hear the door whoof shut, the cracking of a branch as he ran after her. I've told You and told You that I'm getting to the end of my rope, God, and You don't listen.

There was no cover. The man was coming directly to-

ward her, and he had that rifle. He had only to get to a
clear space in the park so he could raise it and aim, and
she was finished.

Janney ran the only way left to her, out onto the golf
course.

Hiding place, she thought. I need a hiding place. I can't
outrun an athletic type like that.

Below the rough the golf course stretched like naked
skin, shaved and exposed.

Oh, God.

She should never have left the church. Better to risk
the dozens of cupboards and cabinets and closets there than
be out here in dark, unfamiliar territory where the gun
would be useful and her legs would not.

Somehow I should double back, she thought. Let him
get out on the golf course while I run back through the
church grounds and get into the church again. Slash his
tires with a knife from the church kitchen. Slash *him* with
a knife from the church kitchen.

The light of the moon was more hint than help: a sense
of being able to see, which was not accompanied by the
proof of feet finding their way.

Running over the rough, which proved true to its name—
full of hillocks, holes, dips, and pits—she remembered the
training stables for the trotters. It was their barbed wire.
That was nice to know. But it didn't give her a place to
run.

She crested the nearest green, stumbled through its
sand trap, and found, wonderfully, a row of thick Meserve
holly bushes. Janney flung herself down in the grass behind them and lay there panting and shaking. Beside her
a cicada rasped. Janney loathed bugs. I have a worse enemy than you, bug, she told it. But don't jump on me.
Especially not on my face. Her fingers touched something
cold and smooth, and she nearly screamed, thinking of
slugs.

The crackling in the woods had stopped. The man would
emerge where she had. He'd be surveying the course, trying
to see her. Had she topped the green before he had a chance

to get out? Or did he know exactly where she was? Was he walking silently over the rough or standing at the edge of the trees?

Janney strained to hear, but the grass was thick. It would give her no warnings. She flattened herself as much as possible and wiggled until she had a ground-level view of the sandpit and the rim of the green above it. Neat, she thought. I'll be able to watch my murderer's feet.

I know him from somewhere. If I could just remember, I'd write it in the sand for the police.

The horrid, smooth, cold thing by her fingers was a golf ball.

Janney held it tightly. A weapon. If David could slay Goliath with a pebble, maybe God would let her use a golf ball to kill a crazy man with a rifle. But Janney had never so much as gotten crushed paper to land in a wastebasket beside her chair. It seemed unlikely that she could use a golf ball to crack the skull of some macho jock with a gun. And if God couldn't even take care of her in a church, He wasn't going to materialize on a golf course.

You remember that part about the still waters and the green pastures, God? she said to Him. Don't pretend you don't see any parallel here. No place has more still waters and green pastures than a golf course. Your part is the rod and the staff. Don't renege.

Janney was struck by the horror that the man had been the one to do the circling. If she turned her head, would he be there, grinning? His rifle pointing at her? Whispering, "Laura?" Chuckling, "Hello, Laura?"

She shuddered, spooked by the name she had not used in thirty-five years. She could not bring herself to look behind her. If she looked, he'd be there. She wanted to dig a hole in the ground, bury herself in the sand from him. She pressed herself so close to the bushes that the leaves pricked a holly pattern in her cheeks.

But all God has ever done is renege, she thought. I prayed to Him for Ross and for Donny and even once or twice, when I was feeling supercharitable, for Avery. And God did nothing. Or then again perhaps we never had a

pact and there was nothing He ever promised that He was
going back on.

She looked behind her.

No human beings. Just a golf course, falling away in a
dim blur of reflected water, white sand, and night-black
grass.

How long have I been here? Forever? Three minutes?
Automatically she tried to look at her watch, but she had
taken it off along with her high heels and left it in the
car, marking the end of her workweek.

What I need here is a periscope, she thought.

She studied the green. An ordinary raised mound of
grass, flat on top. The tip of the flag a bent, quivering
triangle against the slate sky.

She did not know where she was. One of the Holly Oak
Country Club courses, but it had six full eighteen-hole
courses, and there were no handy little plaques telling
her, Yes, Janney, this is course number five, hole number
seventeen, which means your house is...

She ached from the tension of lying down as much as
if she had been painting ceilings for the last twenty-four
hours. *All my bones are out of joint, God, I am poured out
like water.*

I want to go home. I want Ross's room. Full, crowded,
Ross and his things and his music and his talk. Ross before
Avery left, when he wasn't afraid of me and he was be-
ginning to get his act together. Ross laughing and funny.

It came to Janney in a rush of surprise that she needed
Ross more than he needed her. He was all there was left.
If she did not have Ross, there would be nothing to build
around, not one pivot for her life. And I'm too old, she
thought, I'm too tired, to start again. A few years ago I
figured life began at forty, the good years were still waiting. Now I'm aged and sere.

All I ask, God, is that my pivot around Ross cost a little
less. No, that's not all I ask. Get rid of this man with the
rifle.

I can't stand up and look. He's waiting there with his
gun. My forehead will be perforated. I will wait half an

hour. Nobody could possibly be patient for more than half
an hour. He'll give up and leave, and I'll hear his car
engine. Half an hour is 30 minutes times 60 seconds is
1,800 seconds. One space a second, two space a second,
three space a second, four...

There was a telephone at home. A lot of them, as a
matter of fact. Avery had had a jack put in every single
room. The house had far more than it needed of everything,
probably the reason it was so hideously expensive to maintain. She would perch on the stool beside Ross's bed—he
detested anyone's sitting on his mattress—and dial the
police. Ross would be comforting the way he was the other
day when the toaster broke, and together they'd keep calm,
be strong, and plan a move to Alaska. To anyplace as long
as it wasn't Holly Oak. Bad enough to have the memories
she and Ross had, but now some slimy man who knew her
as Laura was crawling around.

Janney felt an almost magnetic tug to get moving toward Ross's room, a place that, unlike the church, was
truly a sanctuary. Had kept Ross safe for years.

She hadn't counted to 100 by the time she was ready
to quit. Counting was certainly a focusing sort of activity.
She felt much more calm. She even rolled on her back and
began to watch the stars as she counted. Lying on her
back, she felt much safer, as if bullets could penetrate only
from behind: 141 space a second, 142 space a second, 143...

I mustn't stop. Patience, have patience. If necessary,
spend the night here.

Frogs chorusing, crickets rasping, locusts yelling, cicadas screaming, birds squawking, something close and
unidentifiable clicking like marbles dropping on wooden
steps. Miscellaneous whirring, crunching, and fluttering.
The only thing that would make her spend the night here
really *was* a bullet in the heart.

By 600 she was leaving out the spacing and just counting.

Fireflies patched the trees over her head with tiny
Christmas-tree sparkles. How Donny had loved fireflies.
Caught them by the jar.

Oh, Donny! thought Janney.

For a moment she thought she would drown in grief. It was like water, coming over her, going up her nostrils, and filling her lungs and choking her.

She had had her life all planned out. Eighteen years for Donny. Fishing in the golf course brook, shopping at the jeans outlet stores for little boys' dungarees reinforced at the knee. Having peanut butter and jelly every noon. Sesame Street coloring books for rainy days. Cutting out gingerbread and building Popsicle-stick cities. Lining up the Matchbox car collection. Oh, God, so traditional, so ordinary, so nice.

God, I would have taken better care of him than You are. Why did You take Donny? Why, why, why?

And then she remembered that she had not taken very good care of him.

She could not lie still any longer. It was impossible; it was too much to ask. The inaction was unbearable.

The fairway sloped down beyond her. If she kept the raised green between her and the church property, it would protect her somewhat. She could run stooped down to the woods on the other side.

And get shot running stooped down to the woods on the other side.

Janney clung to her golf ball.

And a car started up. She listened with incredible relief as the motor caught, a foot revved the engine gently, and the car, manual shift, moved heavily from first gear to second. She lay still until the sound of its motor faded.

Oh, God, he's gone, thank you.

Should she hike home and use her phone or break into the church office? She did not think she could walk into that church again, past those torn banners and broken cabinets. She did not think she could even walk through the woods to get to the church, those dark, crackling woods where the man had stood with his rifle, waiting.

Completely protected by the thick holly bushes, Janney got to her knees. Then, crouching, like someone about to start a race, bouncing a little, retying her sneakers, she started down the fairway. Cutting between two water barriers, she headed for the patch of turpentine slash pines on the far side. Beside them was a grove of thick bushes, perhaps rhododendron, from the full leafiness. She ran hunched, scuttling, like a crab.

Doesn't take long to return to the animal, does it? Janney thought. I heard the man drive away, for heaven's sake. And I'm running for cover. Scurrying like a terrified little beast.

It annoyed Janney to visualize herself. Doubled over, arms hanging like an ape's, blouse torn, left sneaker coming untied. Flopping around a golf course at night.

She stood up, tired of cowering, and he fired at her almost instantly.

Kevin loved waiting.

He knew she was out there, crouching.

He rested against the trunk of a longleaf pine, using a branch to prop the rifle barrel.

In the woods where Kevin hunted deer, there were small, sharp hills and gullies, thick brush, and vines. It was unusual to shoot more than 100 yards. Kevin preferred to shoot offhand or from a kneeling position, and he had never tried prone. Read about it in magazines, but the terrain of the Sandhills didn't lend itself to prone shooting. Belly down, all you got was a face full of poison ivy. The golf course, however, seemed like a fine place to experiment with shooting prone.

Kevin eased silently forward to lie on soft grass at the edge of the rough. He found a long fallen branch to use as a prop this time. After that he merely waited. He had forgotten his uncle. The hunt was like golf or tennis: a match. The woman had more staying power than he'd counted on, and the tougher the competition, the better the game. The predator in Kevin rejoiced.

He didn't spot her until she was 200 or 300 yards down the fairway, running straight, her light-colored blouse a nice target. It was titillating to know she thought she was good enough to run away from him. Kevin sighted carefully, admiring her guts, made allowances for the slight breeze and the drop of the land and the speed at which she was moving, and fired.

She fell like bricks.

Grinning to himself, Kevin swung the rifle casually in an erect position and began walking after her.

He'd killed her instantly because there wasn't a sound out of her. Rory had made all sorts of noises before he stopped breathing.

Kevin had no sling with him and could not merely toss the rifle on his shoulder and let it hang. He'd forgotten how awkward and heavy a gun was to carry when moving. For a moment he was not sure how he'd manage to move the woman's body and still carry the rifle all the way back to Grey's car.

I'll handle it, he thought, enjoying the light breeze that lifted some of the heavy heat off the grass.

The land dipped and rose, and his feet automatically obeyed the course planners' thinking and moved to the left to follow the flow of the fairway. A bunker came between him and his quarry. He skirted it and leaped easily over a brook instead of going down to the golf cart bridge. It was a rule of hunting never to climb a fence or jump a brook when you carried a loaded gun, but Kevin considered that a rule for clumsy jerks with shitty guns. He passed a chinaberry tree draped in honeysuckle. He was surprised the greenskeeper hadn't ripped the vine off. Perhaps the visitors liked it, thought the odor part of the general ambience. Kevin detested the stench.

He came over the rise to where the woman had fallen.

She was not there.

Kevin could not believe it. He'd dropped her perfectly!

Squinting in the faint light, he saw that the sand was pitted and scrabbled, but there was no blood.

He was terribly angry at her for not being there, dead. *He had shot her.* It was like that time with Rory when Kevin said, "I got that deer," and Rory said, "You did not. It got clean away," and they bet on it because Kevin loved collecting bets, but Rory had been right. Kevin had *missed*.

Missed, he thought all morning, listening to Rory's boasting and taunting, thinking of having to pay Rory off. The truth was that Rory was a very poor shot. Sure, he got a deer every season, but he missed fifty. It had never occurred to Rory that he was a bad shot because by definition a man who killed a deer was a good shot. Rory had actually laughed at the idea that Kevin could teach him anything. Laughed and held out his hand for the money Kevin owed him. "For *missing*," taunted Rory.

Kevin had taught him all right. Like William Tell with the apples. "I'm a very good shot," said Kevin quietly. "I could shoot the cap off your head."

"For Christ's sake," said Rory, "you can't hit the side of a barn." Laughing. That same slurpy, superior laugh. And then *yawning*. As if being on a hunt with Kevin, who had missed his deer, were a bore.

And then Rory moved off, shrugging, long and lithe and quiet and graceful, like a deer, and Kevin shot him without even thinking.

It was afterward that he had thought, and the thought was: I'd rather hear that death rattle than that laugh. Taught you a thing or two, didn't I, Rory, old boy?

Kevin stared down the golf course. Nothing moved. That woman! Was she laughing at him somewhere?

His anger congealed and grew cold in his muscles, like metal being forged. In his heart he knew it was his own stupidity that had allowed her to get away. He who believed in the principle of practice makes perfect had attempted a killing shot in utterly foreign conditions: moonlight, great distance, and a new position.

Kevin managed to get out from under his anger. What's the matter with me? he thought. *This is not a game.* She saw me kill Grey. I have to get her before she tells anybody. She'll be hiding behind something. Or under something.

Kevin shook himself. I am not here to have *fun,* he thought.

Kevin's eyes swiveled, looking for a hiding place, and he caught movement far down the fairway. Now he could see her! Running, rising up a bit and then dipping under a tree and vanishing from his sight.

God, the woman could move!

Adrenaline. That was why it was best to shoot your deer unaware, before it got all that extra energy from fear. Energy that could carry it, even with a gutful of lead, out of your reach.

She, like Rory, was something of a fool. Running down the golf course lacked logic. Following a path lacked logic. She should be hiding. Kevin assumed she was too frightened to hide. She was just going to charge along, and he, Kevin, would run faster, run better, and take her before she reached the next hole.

Like golf, he thought, bending forward and running, enjoying his muscles and the way his lungs never tired. "I'll give her a hole in one," he whispered into the wind. "Right in the heart."

And it was fun.

CHAPTER
NINE

PERSONALLY Janney would not have picked a town where'd she have to spend her retirement panting.

North Carolina in summer was not comfortable, and golfers were less comfortable than most. The local theory was that the sand under the bent-grass fairways would not retain heat, so the earth would cool more rapidly in the Sandhills than elsewhere, and night temperatures would therefore be comfortable.

Janney felt this depended on your standards of comfort.

What it was out there on the golf course was hot.

She had considered the course a flat, manicured, indeed boring stretch of greenery.

She was wrong on all counts. By night it was black. The turf that looked so innocuous from her kitchen window turned out to be full of subtle slants and unexpected dips. The fairway that seemed to move directly toward the mounded green in the distance curved, sloped, and meandered. It was sprinkled with trees that seemed to be composed of low-hanging branches with no trunks. Wooden stakes emerged from the ground like buckteeth wanting to bite her ankles. Sandpits puckered everything, but at least they were white in the moonlight and posed no threat.

Or so she thought until she discovered a sandpit hidden by a miniature bluff and fell eighteen inches knee first into the broken spike of an old wooden tee. Her falling was accompanied by a tremendous noise, as if she had fallen through glass onto rock. Dizzied, Janney pulled the tee out of her skin. It hurt, but it wasn't bleeding much. She put a hand out to help push herself up and found a plastic sand rake handle under her fingers.

It was someone else's car starting up, she thought. I am so stupid that never even occurred to me. That noise was the report of the rifle. *He's still out there.* Shooting at me.

She decided she had better things to do than rake the sand smooth for the next golfer. She began to run.

Janney preferred sedentary pleasures. She had not done any running since compulsory track tests in high school phys. ed. classes. She was filled with admiration at the way each forward-thrusting left leg was succeeded by an even quicker-moving right leg, thus propelling her ahead. But not propelling her fast enough. She was sauntering when she needed to fly.

She looked back once and saw nobody, nothing, and somehow that was even more terrifying than his shape would have been. Bullets were coming out of the formless dark to get her.

No, keep calm, only one bullet and it had missed; she had only to keep running.

Keep running? thought Janney. When I'm so out of shape, I'm not sure if I can even keep breathing?

How retarded I am. Attracting a roadside maniac, wandering into a deserted church, and now progressing down a vacant golf course.

She could not believe she had gotten herself into such an insane predicament.

Being called Laura was like being pursued by her own ghost.

It was not surprising that the Sandhills would contain so much sand near at hand, but Janney had never guessed how much water there was as well. Tiny rills turned out to be too wide to jump. Reflecting pools did not reflect because she could not see them, owing to the tricky lie of the land, until she had to brake like a cartoon creature to keep from running right into the water. The bridges she located lacked rails or sides, and one of them, to her horror, lacked middle planks.

She would have liked to meditate on this conundrum (what manner of trap did the golf course designer have in mind? Or was it vandalism? Or a minidrawbridge?), but there was no time.

She came upon a split-rail fence, the sort that is stacked at oblique angles and used to border the yards of historic houses. At the speed Janney was traveling, it actually seemed logical to gallop right over it, with a great horsey leap, but it occurred to her that she had no idea what sat behind this fence, and as it was the first such obstacle she had met, possibly it was supposed to tell her something.

Like—don't.

She did not look back again. She could feel the presence of the crazy man, ballooning and murderous, and if she saw him as well, she was afraid she would give up. She zigzagged, but it was not on purpose to avoid bullets. The golf course forced it upon her.

Ahead of her was a building. Barnlike, its roof sloped in angles that would make a nice silhouette photograph. Its decks shelved out over the rough. Neat shrubbery made dark speckled areas around a flatness that was either a large lake or a parking lot.

A Halfway House.

Perhaps the place had a resident manager, or summer workers in a bunkroom, or restaurant staff cleaning up after a late Saturday night crowd, all of whom would spring to her aid. Janney ran, panting, gasping, her whole body burning, up the interminable slope to the flatness beyond the bushes. It was a parking lot, and it was empty.

Where are all the good Samaritans now when I need them? she thought. I'd be glad to see even a few bad Samaritans.

The utilities were evidently underground because there were no telephone poles. There seemed to be no pay phone. She ran to the door of the entry pavilion, which in winter was a warm, welcoming glass house, and in summer a furnace. It was locked.

Inside, Janney could see a jungle of plants on a quarry tile floor with steps leading up to the carpeted foyer. Bathrooms, cafeteria, vending machines, shower rooms, and equipment rental offices spread from there. I could break the glass, she thought. I even have a golf ball in my pocket to do it with.

She had never broken into anything, or considered it, in her life. Some things you have to do, Janney told herself, feeling very tough, and she wrapped her hand in her skirt, smashed a pane with the ball, and reached in to turn the door handle.

It did not turn. Locked on the inside as well. *God,* she said.

She could either give up or break enough panes to walk in. Each pane was divided by a small rectangle of wood. Janney looked behind her and felt the presence of the man with the rifle. Suddenly it seemed easy to kick in the door.

She tapped lightly with her sneaker, not wanting to shred her leg with glass shards. Nothing broke. She kicked harder, and that didn't accomplish anything either. Finally she took the golf ball again and began methodically smashing the little mitered joints of the glass frames. At the fourth broken joint she cut her hand.

Musicians, especially keyboard musicians, are very protective of their fingers. Pianists have been known to learn to play the sousaphone so as to be able to substitute marching band for the gym requirement at college. (In gym there is always a good possibility of damaging one's fingers.) Indeed, Janney had dated a harpsichordist who refused to play tennis for fear of tennis elbow, and he in turn was quite understanding that Janney never served cabbage salad or cheese soufflé because in the shredding of the food she might remove the tip of a finger.

Janney looked at her hand and the spurting blood, and she knew immediately she had cut a tendon as well as flesh. Hurting her hand was far more frightening to Janney than being shot at. She doubled her skirt around the cut, but it did not stop the bleeding. I need to tie something tightly around it, she thought. I could take off my blouse.

But even with her life in danger that was beyond her. Liberated matron, huh! thought Janney. Bet Gloria Steinem would take off her blouse. Sobbing, Janney ran around the Halfway House, looking for another door, a cracked window. Phone! I have to have a phone, she thought.

The lower back door was open. She had only to walk in.

Janney groped for lights, turned them on, and ran for a bathroom. The men's room appeared first, so that was where she went. Inside, she grabbed paper towels—thank God, the soft white kind, not the harsh brown variety—and wrapped her hand in them. Pressing hard, she stopped the blood flow, the pain, and some of the fear. The fear she had now was of removing her right hand, whose grip contained the pain and the blood.

She stood there, gasping, thinking of her hand, of plastic surgery, of what she would do if her left fingers no longer responded the way that she wanted them to. But what difference, really, would it make? Her customers wouldn't notice if she amputated the whole damn hand. Besides, the dreadful little machines she sold threw the chords in by themselves.

I should make a market along those lines, Janney thought. All one-armed would-be musicians, get your organs here!

She had been on the library board a few years ago, when Grey Randallman was chairman. They'd had to hire a new librarian and were staggered when a representative of the Equal Opportunity Commission showed up to address the board. It seemed that equal consideration was to be given to hiring black, handicapped, Native American, Puerto Rican (if there was a single Hispanic in the Sandhills, he was well disguised), male, female, elderly, and both under- and overqualified applicants. Considering that absolutely nobody in the entire United States of America seemed to want to be a librarian in Holly Oak, it was ludicrous to suppose the board had hundreds of applicants through which it could sift, eagerly keeping its prejudices at bay. After the meeting Grey rapped his gavel very solemnly and said to the board, "Ladies, gentlemen, I want y'all to scour the countryside. We are lookin' for a one-legged septuagenarian Indian woman librarian."

It had become a password for them. Whenever Janney met a religious friend in Holly Oak, the friend was sure to mention prayer in time of trouble; whenever she met a fellow suffering board member, he'd whisper furtively, "Spotted any one-legged Indian women yet?"

She started to smile. Grey Randallman was such a—Grey.

It was Grey's car. Long, huge, with a silvery top. A red '57 Cadillac, an astonishing, laugh-provoking relic of an-other age, of which Grey was enormously proud. She could not think why she had not known the car in her rearview mirror instantly. What other car in the whole state re-sembled it? My car is so low, she thought, that I couldn't see that silvered top, and it was too dark to distinguish the red and the fins. And besides, I'm so hyped up on coffee and depression I probably shouldn't be allowed to drive.

A young man, she thought. Driving Grey's car. Chasing me.

Grey had a nephew. Janney vaguely remembered read-ing something about him. Whatever she'd read had gone the way of all things not related to her personal prob-lems—vanished into the void.

Grey's nephew chasing her? But that was impossible. Grey was the most civilized man Janney knew. His nephew—no, the car must have been stolen, that was it. Perhaps she had seen the theft. The other man, the one with his back to her—but what about the truck? There had been writing on the truck, but Janney barely managed to read stop signs, let alone company names on parked trucks. She thought: But what could—

A door creaked.

She'd left the lights on, like the jerk she was, as if she were the keeper of the beacons on Hatteras. Here, crazy man, come and get me!

There was no place to hide in the men's room. The place

had a gaudy, bright, white-tiled sterility that hurt her eyes as much as the glass hurt her hand.

Another door opened and, in a moment, closed.

Janney slid to the edge of the men's room, turned off the lights, and moved back into one of the toilet cubicles. She stood on the toilet, so her feet wouldn't show if he came in and turned on the lights, and then stooped, so her head and shoulders wouldn't stick up above the gray metal dividers. It was a precarious position. The toilet rim sloped.

Water hazards wherever I go, she thought, fighting back the edge of hysteria.

She steadied herself with her good hand, making a fist out of her damaged left hand, hoping the blood wouldn't start dripping on the floor.

Or had it already? Were there big red splotches on the immaculate white tile?

In spite of His previous poor record, she mentioned her troubles to God again. However, if He was unresponsive in the church, the green pastures, and the still waters, He was unlikely to show up in a men's room.

She heard another door open. The footsteps were very close, ghostly, whispering. In the ladies' room, she thought, right next to the men's room. The plumbing chase must be behind me. She could hear him opening every cubicle door. It was eerie feeling the slight thud of each door as it swung shut again.

The bathrooms had been designed to save space. Tall men probably learned to go at home if they valued their kneecaps. The doors opened outward into a little mirrored passage because there wasn't room between the door and the commode to swing a door inward.

In the dark she told herself he wouldn't look in a men's room for an uptight matron who couldn't even use her blouse for a bandage.

He came into the men's room and turned on the lights.

The gray metal between her and the rifle was pitiful. She almost wanted to give up and get it over with.

His shoes tapped on the tile. He opened the door of the first cubicle.

Janney huddled in the second.

She held her breath, prayed, and lunged into the metal door with her full weight, the first time her extra seven pounds had ever seemed an asset. The door and Janney crashed outward into the man's face, knocking him backward onto the tile wall. She fell on top of him, and he grabbed at her. Janney got hold of the middle of his rifle and crammed it in his already bloody face.

She was staring into a pair of wild eyes, a broken nose, and a cupful of blood. She expected the man never to let go of her, to be locked in this terrible position until dawn or her death, whichever came first, but he cried out and put both hands to his smashed nose. Janney freed herself and ran, scrambling and slipping, out of the men's room, while the crazy man roared after her.

"Laura!" he screamed, cursing her horridly. It was the first time she'd heard swear words used as if they weren't merely poor language or repetitive exclamations but genuine curses. As though he truly intended that she be damned for fighting back. She was almost glad it was Laura he was damning; it seemed, ridiculously, to give Janney a measure of safety from the curses.

She ran back the way she'd come. The golf course was horrible, but the building, with that man roaring like a demented lion, was worse.

She heard him slamming doors, yelling, swearing, and while he was satisfying himself with the racket, she slid very carefully out of the building and over to the azalea bed. After burrowing into the copious branches, she lay on the wood-chip mulch, splinting her hurt hand against her hipbone.

CHAPTER
TEN

WHEN SHE FLED THE BUILDING, she let the door slam.

Kevin wanted to crunch her, smash her between two solid objects.

She'd gotten him right in the nose, right at the bridge. It was bleeding as if she had knifed him. He had to stop to gather up paper towels; the blood was coming so fast it oozed into his mouth when he took a breath. He crammed the towels against his face, picked up the rifle, and went after her, turning off lights as he went. He'd kill her now! He had meant to kill her anyway, but now he would *really* kill her.

The pain from his nose saturated his entire skull, blending with the bump on the back where he'd struck the tile wall. What if his nose healed crooked?

He ran upstairs and out onto the deck that encircled the Halfway House to survey the golf course. She was gone. He had lost her. Rage consumed Kevin, mingling with the pain and the humiliation, until he thought he would rather kill her with his hands than his rifle. His hands were shaking not from nerves, but from feelings of wrath crawling down to his extremities. The tic returned to his cheek. The *idea* that some stupid middle-aged *woman* could defy him like this! Inflict pain, damage him! And then *get away from him!* He wanted to rip her hair the way he had the flags. He wanted to scalp her.

Kevin went back indoors. He knew the Halfway House

well, having had several hundred grilled cheese sand-
wiches and Dr Peppers there. Back in the lobby, the telephones were on the desk in a neat little row, and at night
the desk was enclosed by a grillwork that lowered and was
padlocked. She wasn't going to use those at any rate.

So where would she find a phone? She'd have to—

And he remembered the purse. The silly stuffed purse
with the embroidered elephant and the four little metal
feet. He'd read her name off the license: Laura J. Fraser,
white, female, 135, 5–5, 211 Mashie Lane, Holly Oak,
North Carolina. She lived just on the other side of the golf
course. In fact, of all the houses that ringed the club, hers
was one of the closest.

Kevin began running back toward the church and Grey's
car, taking turns with each hand at carrying the rifle and
massaging his nose. At the church he paused to get the
woman's key ring out of her car. Good. Yes. Obviously a
front door key on the ring.

His rage consumed him. He had forgotten the truck
stuck in the sand and the deer stiffening in the woods. He
had forgotten the corpse of his uncle in the trunk and the
necessity to flee. He had a great capacity for emotions, but
for only one at a time. Right now it was rage.

Nobody beat Kevin Clary. Certainly not some bitch his
mother's age.

As he drove, he fished around in the brown paper shopping bag from the hunting supply store. He slipped two
full boxes of shells into his pocket. Like to riddle her damn
body, he thought, his fingers white on the steering wheel.
He took the curves savagely, wildly, as if he were driving
over Laura. Breaking my *nose,* he thought. *My* nose!

Janney could not believe he had not seen her lying there
in the azaleas, shielded from anyone facing her, but totally
exposed to someone like him, looking down from above. It
was not possible to know whether God, luck, or shadows
had hidden her.

Janney watched the man trot back down the golf course
the way he had come. She got to her knees and watched

him get smaller and smaller, a vague pencil in the moonlight. Going back to his car, she thought. He can't hide on me this time. I *saw* him leave this time.

She went into the Halfway House by the door he'd left open. The telephones were behind a locked grille. God, said Janney, I do not believe this.

How was she supposed to get the police? How was she supposed to accomplish anything? It was going to be like all her other problems. In the end, in the goddamned end, she was going to have to do it all herself, and that meant she would screw up—it was the story of her life.

She stared bleakly at a little stand on which a laminated colored map of the courses of Holly Oak Country Club was displayed. "YOU ARE HERE," it said, with an arrow pointing toward the Halfway House. The map was charming, with little drawings of each sassafras tree or water fountain and darling quail covies decorating the open areas. It did not give the names of the streets that stuck their cul-de-sac fingers down into the neatly maneuvered hills and pools. After some figuring, Janney established that she was a six-hole walk to the end of this course (the other three holes doubled back), and then, after crossing the parking lots and Deep River Road again, she'd have to cross three more holes and she'd be in her own backyard.

Home.

She wanted home so fiercely it hurt more than her hand.

She could not take her tired eyes off the silent cream-colored telephones on the tiled counter top. She needed a telephone so much! There had to be a pay phone somewhere that was not locked up.

There wasn't.

Okay, she told herself. You can walk home and phone from there. Just keep calm. Remember how to act like Todd's liberated matron.

She decided to take the golf cart route. For that matter, she thought, I could take a golf cart.

Under the circumstances the trustees of the club would surely not prosecute.

The golf carts sat in a little pen, like docile corralled

animals, facing outward for another day. Sunday would
be their big day; perhaps they were resting up for it. They
were electric and appeared to be startable with the little
keys left in them. How thoughtful of the management.

But the pen itself was locked. She could drive around
inside it like Disney World, bumping other golf carts and
shrieking with glee, but she couldn't get out of the pen.

Janney kicked the pen gate in frustration, and to her
astonishment the flimsy gate sagged on its hinges and
came off. That didn't seem the sort of thing God would do,
so it must be luck.

She sat on a cart, started it up, and it began trundling
forward with only slight pressure from her right foot. She
passed a sign on which golf rules were posted: Slower groups
must allow faster groups to play through, no liquor allowed
on the course. Right, Janney promised, count on me.

She trundled down the soft slope under the deck where
the man with the rifle had stood, the golf cart purring like
a satisfied tomcat.

Ross woke with a start, surprised that he had slept at
all. He hadn't pressed the buttons that lowered his hospital
bed; he was still slumped half erect on the pillows. If she'd
come home, Janney would have lowered the bed and fixed
the sheets. She never went upstairs without checking on
him first. Ross strained to see out into the dark yard.
Usually she left the car right by the front steps instead of
going on into the carport. He could see no glitter of chrome
or glass in the moonlight.

He looked at his watch. *One-forty.*

Ross caught his breath. She'd had an accident then.
Something had gone wrong on those empty, endless
stretches of country she liked to drive through. She could
be anywhere.

He picked up the telephone to call the village police
and then set it down. Janney would hate his interference.
"I can handle it myself," she said all the time, when he
could see her hand trembling, see that the last thing on

earth she wanted was to handle it by herself. She wanted
Avery to be there to handle it for her.

If she'd had car trouble, she would want to prove to
herself that she could cope. And how would she do that?
Walk up to some darkened house where God only knew
what kind of person lived? And what if she were hurt and
couldn't cope?

He lifted the phone again.

But the distance between the mall where she worked
to Holly Oak was three counties. Probably at least five or
six different sheriff and police departments had jurisdic-
tion in between.

Ross set the phone down again to think.

Maybe he should give her until 2:00 A.M. to show. Except
that if she were physically hurt, every second would matter.

He was acting like the Gothic heroine in one of the
paperbacks the bookmobile librarian sometimes insisted
on leaving with him. The girl always had a stupid name,
Mignonette or Aprille, and she spent half of each chapter
trying to make decisions. Just like me, thought Ross. I
should do this, but if I do that, then this might happen
and reactions might be unfavorable, but if I don't because
then—And the books were surpassingly boring. I could
write a better book than that, he would think in disgust.
If there's one thing I know firsthand, it's being helpless.

So he would call the village police and ask them what
to do, a course of action invariably overlooked by each pea-
brained Gothic heroine.

Ross reached for the telephone a third time, and as his
arm moved through the dark to the bedside table, he heard
someone in the living room gasping for breath.

Catherine Randallman got into her Buick and drove
past her sister-in-law's. Grey's car was not there. Kevin's
car was in the driveway. When she banged on the door,
nobody answered. She drove slowly through the village.
No scarlet 1957 Caddy.

Grey loved that car. Splashy, gaudy, pretentious, os-

tentatious, dated, gas-guzzling—and absolutely marvel-
ous, he said. He planned to keep driving the Caddy until
the world ran out of gasoline. Tomorrow was Sunday, and
every Sunday morning since 1957 Grey had washed his
car, drying it lovingly out of direct sunlight, using a Q-
tip to clean dirt from the cracks. There were a number of
times when Catherine felt she occupied second place to
the Caddy.

Grey had said something last week about going up to
his land in Randolph County. The property was ugly scrub
country: no views, no attractions. She'd driven down Deep
River Road and past the weedy, rutted lane a thousand
times, but she doubted if she'd actually turned into the
property more than twice in thirty years.

Grey went more often. Hunted there, she told herself,
although she felt a faint twinge. *You know better,* said the
twinge. Could he and Kevin have gone up there? Night
hunting? Coon hunting?

She thought of what had happened to Rory, who went
hunting with Kevin. It was an accident, she told herself.
The police never brought charges. It was an accident. *You
know better,* said the twinge.

Maybe both Kevin and Grey had had an accident. Car
accident.

But Kevin had been in trouble before Grey arrived.

She had no place else to look. She turned north on Deep
River Road.

When Janney came over the next rise, the land opened
out in front of her, and she could see the Holly Oak water
tower. It was shaped like a golf ball on a tee. Painted on
the white surface of the huge globe were pale gray circles
intended to resemble the dented surface of a real golf ball.
The huge supporting tee and ladders were painted gaudy
yellow. Across the ball, in enormous black script, were the
words *Holly Oak Country Clubs.*

Of all the blights on the landscape, the water tower was
Janney's personal hate. A good honest ugly water tower
was acceptable. A bloated golf ball was not.

She buzzed along the path, leaving the golf ball behind, and ahead of her was a single street light marking the road which separated course number three from course number four. Almost home.

Years ago, returning home from college freshman year, she'd felt like this: an almost nauseating relief that homesickness was about to be terminated; as soon as the plane landed, she'd be safe. Home.

The existence of the road registered in her brain. It was the same road the church was on. The crazy man had gone back, presumably to get Grey's car. Would he expect her to come out on this road? He could very well be just out of sight, lights off, motor off, ready to pounce on her when she came under the light by the curb.

Janney took her foot off the accelerator, and the little cart hummed like a hovering bee. Home was only three holes away, but the road now seemed like an unbridgeable chasm between her and safety. Her hand was bleeding again. A crowd of tiny gnats began collecting around it, landing on the blood-soaked paper towels. Janney shook her hand to get rid of them and for the first time felt a searing pain. Immediately she was doubled over, moaning, protecting the cut hand with the fold of her waist.

Down the road a car was approaching.

She pressed the accelerator of the cart and aimed for a copse of young dogwoods, whose fat leaves draped to form a thin green sheet. Golf carts are not speed demons. Shoving her foot down merely made the cart lurch, and its wheels churned up an unforgivable mess in the turf.

The automobile's engine was loud, whacking with missed beats, backfiring like a rifle. She debated getting off the cart as one debates abandoning ship. If she left the cart out here, its white body and orange and white striped sunshade under the pool of lamplight would be seen by anyone. Her maniac would know the cart had no business being out at this hour.

Makes it sound like an escaped goat, thought Janney. She slipped under the dogwoods, rammed a thin vulnerable trunk, and got her foot off the pedal. She was in a damp place, and tree frogs, locusts, and crickets were screeching, scratching, and singing. The soft electric hum of her cart blended in like pedal point in a Victorian organ work.

She stared out between two dogwood branches. It was a badly tuned pickup truck. The cab appeared to have two adults and a baby standing up between them. Janney leaped off her cart and ran after them, signaling, but there were thornbushes between her and the road: a thick hedge of wild rose sprouting enough thorns to pierce an army. By the time she realized the bushes were impassable and the only way off the golf course was via the golf cart path, the pickup truck was long gone.

Janney stood by the road, shaking. Her hand hurt terribly. She had all the strength of a used Kleenex. Was this how Ross felt?

Janney panted from heat, fear, pain, and exhaustion. Okay, God, let's cross this street. If you can part the Red Sea, you ought to be able to guide a golf cart.

She could not walk the rest of the way home. She could scarcely totter back to the cart. Having unlaced her sneakers with one hand, she kicked them off and then, awkwardly, peeled off her thick white sports socks. Dropping the wad of paper towels to the ground, Janney pulled a sock over the cut hand, turning the cuff up to make another blood-absorbing layer of bandage. The second sock she tugged over the first.

When she got her sneakers back on, she could no longer lace them since her left hand was a fingerless mitt. The shoes sat in loose puddles around her feet. She backed the cart out of the dogwoods and onto the path again.

After steering across the road, Janney entered the next golf course as if General Patton had ordered her to cross minefields, hunching her shoulders, trying to look inconspicuous. Like Ross the first year, she thought, trying to pretend that wasn't really him in the wheelchair. She followed the long, winding dogleg to its oblique turn, and when the cart was entirely out of sight of the road, she was almost giddy with relief. Ahead of her stretched a ridiculous number of sand traps and bunkers. Truly a golf course was a peculiar place. If one were excavated 2,000 years from now, what would an archaeologist think of people who entertained themselves by pockmarking their lawns?

The sounds of the night ceased to be part of the chase and turned into music. Mendelssohn at his sprightliest, Janney thought. Not the organ music, that's never sprightly. Perhaps *Midsummer Night's Dream.*

Fireflies sprinkled the air like miniature clear Christmas-tree bulbs on a Mary Poppins adventure. There was a Hindemith piece, full of murmuring gongs and orchestral whispers, that always made her think of an Oriental Cinderella rushing out of the palace at midnight. This is the setting, she thought, as the piece chased Mendelssohn out of her mind.

I met the enemy and vanquished him, she thought. Well, not exactly vanquished, but gave him a bloody nose and got away alive. That's pretty vanquished in my book. I wonder what it indicates that my victorious steed is a golf cart, whose ability to move depends on a dimmer switch.

She began to feel cocky. The shivering Hindemith was replaced by a triumphal fanfare of brass chorus.

Imagine me, the typical half-pasted-together musician, wheeling down a golf course in the small hours, fresh from a confrontation with Evil.

Janney steered neatly around a curve and up over a tiny bridge, thinking how Donny would love the cart. He'd want to steer and take little side excursions and see if the sunshade was strong enough for him to bounce on.

From the brush on her left came a shudder of movement. Janney froze in horror, her foot falling off the accelerator, the little cart slowing. The bushes parted. Oh, God, thought Janney, tears of fear stabbing her eyes again. Oh, please, no, I can't—

It was a rabbit.

The gurgle of horrified laughter that spouted from her throat frightened the rabbit more than the cart, and it leaped off in long white-flashing bounds, ears back, body close to the ground.

Donny had wanted a rabbit once. *Can I have a bunny, Mommy? Please can I have a bunny?* Avery got him a pair, announcing that Donny could breed them and sell them and begin learning about capitalism. The rabbits, however, proved much harder to breed than Avery expected, given rabbit PR. Not only did Donny never earn a dime, but Avery had to dole out constant allowances to buy the rabbit feed. What he's learning about, said Ross, grinning, is government subsidy. Avery had not been amused.

I can laugh about it, Janney thought. Oh, God, yes, let me laugh.

She could see Donny with his hammer, making his ridiculous road crosses and leaning them up against every tree, so proud of his street signs.

She had no tears left for Donny. Just memories. For the first time since Donny's death, she was coming home smiling.

CHAPTER
ELEVEN

Ross would have said there was a limit to how helpless a man could feel. He was paralyzed, weak, dizzy, taken care of by a stepmother, had no money, no future, and no friends. You couldn't get more helpless than that.

Now he knew he was wrong.

Oh, God, he thought, it gets worse?

He did not find it incredible. Few unpleasant things were beyond belief to Ross. He lay unmoving, listening to the breathing.

A burglar.

And not one thing he could do about it. Ah, God, to have legs. To be able to jump up and stomp on the guy. Wrestle him down. Tie him up first and call the cops second.

Ross just lay there.

In the next room the breathing became less labored, more relaxed. The burglar was beginning to move around. Exploring.

This is the dining room, thought Ross. Bet he'll go upstairs for the jewels and the cash and come back down here for the silver.

Janney had sold the silver. They'd done something right for a change, hitting the highest week on the fluctuating silver market. She'd wanted to buy a van like Peter's so she could take Ross on trips. Ross could go in the Pinto, but he wasn't comfortable sitting up for more than a short time, and there was no way to put a mattress in a compact car. But the van cost too much, and the bank turned Janney down for a loan, pointing out that she had a lot of liabilities and only one asset, the house, which could not be transferred without Avery's signature.

Neighbors insisted that 100 percent disabled vets were eligible for "tons" of government money. Ross didn't doubt that he was eligible. But being eligible and actually getting the money were two different things. He had a pension which covered the cost of his aides. It did not support Janney or the too-large, heavily mortgaged house Avery had bought them.

The footsteps moved toward the stairs. If he comes in here, I'll have to pretend to be asleep, thought Ross. He didn't need to pretend. Sleep was the only thing he did well. He always looked asleep.

The burglar was wearing very heavy shoes, which surprised Ross. He'd have expected rubber soles at the very least, even stockinged feet. Once the man was upstairs, the steps seemed to come from hitherto-unknown spaces. Janney never walks in the room where the burglar is now, Ross thought. I haven't heard sounds up there since Donny died.

Treading in Donny's room, where even he, Ross, could not trespass. Ross wanted to bellow like a bull: *Get out of my house.* But he should make no threats he could not carry out, and a trapped burglar might be a dangerous adversary.

Trapped, he thought. As if I could trap somebody. Or be an adversary. I'll have to lie here like the infant I am and wait it out. This will destroy Janney. She's been waiting for the last straw. She comes in the door tonight and—

And where was she?

What woke me up? Ross thought. He shifted in the bed, pulling himself forward until he could peer around the corner of the house and see the head of the driveway. Filling the entrance, mostly hidden by shrubs and trees, was a large gleaming shape that looked more like an operating table than a car.

But it must be his car, thought Ross. And how did he get in? Surely I'd have heard him if he broke in. I know the aide locked up. I reminded her. I heard her.

The footsteps were coming down. Heavily and quickly. A sort of carefree step. The man had found the bedrooms empty and figured he was alone in the house.

I don't even have a weapon, thought Ross. Nothing hard, nothing rough, nothing pointed. And I can't break bricks with my hand. I can hardly turn a radio dial.

He braced himself, but the burglar did not enter the dining room. Through the opened door Ross could see a bit of the breakfast corner of the kitchen, and the burglar actually strolled in and sat in a chair there, something Ross had never done, so he couldn't guess whether the burglar was comfortable, and then there was silence.

Ross was more mystified than frightened. Why would you sneak into a house in order to sit at the breakfast table?

Using the rope that hung from the ceiling joist, Ross carefully pulled himself forward in the bed until he could see more of the kitchen corner. The moonlight showed him only a silhouette. A man. One hand on his face, as if massaging a headache. A man not sufficiently interested in the prospect of dining room treasure to enter the dining room. A man who wanted to be sure the bedrooms held no sleepers. A man, furthermore, with a rifle in his right hand.

The man set the rifle on the table, lying across the two quilted place mats, and opened the window. It creaked a bit, but it went up for him. He took the rifle in his hand again and dropped the muzzle on the sill, the butt resting on his knees.

There was nothing out there but a strip of wood and a golf course. A few rabbits, the odd woodchuck and raccoon, maybe a stray dog.

A sniper? he thought. In our kitchen? A rifle?

And Janney late.

Ross had a number of ways to communicate with the outside: the telephone, the ham radio, a citizens' band radio, an intercom, and a bell. But there weren't fifteen feet between him and the man with the rifle, and none of his instruments worked in silence. Nor did his voice.

The bell was something Avery had rigged up so Ross could summon Janney when she was out of doors and could not hear his call. It rang, as she had specified, the traditional ding-dong. I don't like those buzzy ones, she'd said darkly. She used to call Donny in the same pitch that the doorbell rang in—*Donnn-eeeee*—a falling minor third. It's a worldwide human trait, Ross, she told him once, the whole world calls people in minor thirds.

But the bell wasn't sufficiently loud to alert neighbors, even if any had been in residence, and Janney, if she came, would interpret it as a signal that Ross needed help, not that she should stay away.

He definitely could not use the ham transmitter. The static and racket and clicking were second only to CB. He could pull the phone to him in silence, as it was on a rotating shelf, but it was not push-button; it still had the old-fashioned dial, and the man could not help hearing the seven partial turns, not to mention Ross's voice asking for the police.

And when the man noticed Ross, by sound or sight, Ross would find out what that rifle was for. And Ross had already had experience with weaponry. He grabbed the cord he used to exercise by, planning to shift position, and was immediately seized by a headache.

They weren't really headaches since the pain was systemic. The doctors explained that metal fragments too small to search out were still lodged in his brain and skull. Ross pictured them as splinters working their way to the surface, slicing his brain as they went, gathering beneath his skull to pierce the bone.

Listening, thinking, moving, and functioning became academic. There was nothing in Ross but the attempt to reach a sort of mental fetal position, to splint the agony. It rarely worked. Ross gritted his teeth, sending the pain into his jaw, attacking his eyes from the bottom. He managed to lean back on the pillows without crying out.

The headache spread. Now his chest hurt, so that breathing, perfectly ordinary breathing, cut his nerves.

The man in the kitchen said, "Okay, Laura. I see you. Got yourself transportation, didn't you? Clever girl. But you're not getting away this time, you bitch. I'll shoot you between the eyes, baby."

The venom in the voice jolted right past Ross's pain. *Laura?* The rifle was for *Laura,* coming from the golf course?

Ross doubted if anyone besides Avery and the IRS knew that Janney Fraser was really Laura J. Fraser. Even at the wedding the minister had said: Do you, Janney, take this man . . . Taken him and lived to regret it, thought Ross.

He was planning to shoot *Janney* between the eyes?

He pushed away the communications equipment. There was no time for that, even supposing he could get away with the noise it would make. Nor could Ross overpower anyone. He certainly could achieve nothing by trying to tangle with a rifle.

His wheelchair was next to the bed. Slowly and carefully Ross removed the rustling sheets that covered his legs. He got himself into position and took a good grip on the rope. The house was too quiet. He could not get into the chair in absolute silence. In the grip of a headache like this he might lose his balance, miss the chair, hit the table.

Ross reached behind his bed for the thermostat and turned the cooling gauge down to sixty. Instantly the air conditioning came on with a surging whir. Ross swung himself off the bed and lowered his body the two inches into the wheelchair. He did not have a battery-operated chair. Whenever he felt good enough to be up, he felt good enough to pull the wheels. He took the armrests off the table where they were kept between uses—it was difficult to get in and out with the armrests in the way—and pushed them back down.

The downstairs was carpeted in a tight commercial-grade weave since Ross could not have propelled the chair over deep nap or shag. There were no door ledges, and none of the openings was too narrow for the chair. The only obstacle was a man with a rifle.

Ross turned around the foot of the bed. He was looking directly into the breakfast room. The man might be ten feet away. His back to Ross, he was leaning forward, staring into the darkness that spread off the back of the house, running his hand down the shaft of the rifle.

Ross went down the hall and into the living room. The furniture was placed for his maneuvering, and he and Janney never had company to pose conversational problems because of distant seats, so it was easy to steer through the shadowy house. The wheelchair was one thing, at least, he could maintain in good operating condition. It neither squeaked nor rattled.

His usual exit was the ramp at the kitchen door, but for safety's sake there was another at the French doors in the living room. The doors had to be unbolted first, and Ross was afraid they would scrape. In the kitchen the man shifted his seat, and the chair legs scraped on the tile. The guy began tapping impatiently. It was a nice rhythmic tap. Ross timed his bolt sliding for the taps. Opened them both, slid the doors open, and rolled down the ramp. The trouble with this way out was that Ross could not close the doors himself. By the time he was over the threshold the doors were impossible for him to reach back and close. But it was a hot and nearly windless night. Perhaps they wouldn't bang shut. They'd create quite a draft, though. The air conditioner would never go off.

The only path toward the course was one Avery had put in, leading from the kitchen door and meandering across the yard in full view of the man with the rifle. In a wheelchair Ross could hardly strike off through the grass, skulking behind shrubs and trees as if it were Vietnam. Ross maneuvered between two thick bridal wreath bushes.

For a better view at mealtime, Avery had cleared out the woods between his yard and the rough. Avery had loved the location of his house, loved every golfer he was privileged to watch, loved every little white ball that landed in his yard and threatened his guests.

And I *hate* this lousy house, thought Ross. How come *he's* the one who got to leave?

Ross tried to see the golf course, but he was too low. In the moonlight he could not even see past the dim forms of the shrubs.

The muzzle of the rifle came out the window and steadied.

Off the golf course he heard the low buzz of an electric motor.

"Janney!" screamed Ross. "Janney, *go back!*"

I am alive, thought Grey Randallman.

But how can that be?

The pain was enormous. It splintered and banged on him. It roared and rocked. How could pain be noisy? Grey could perceive nothing except that he was hurt and that he was alive. There seemed to be no way to progress beyond that; he was being flung around in some casket of agony.

And then it stopped. Through the pain came a final crash and then silence. Just Grey and pain. No more noise, no more flinging. He panted. He tried to locate himself, even to the simple act of touching himself, but he seemed not to be able to control his body. If I'm alive, and if I hurt, I have fingers, he thought. I have arms. I should be able to—

But he could do nothing except quiver as the pain coursed over him.

Ross screaming? thought Janney. *Janney, go back!*

Ross, who never raised his voice because that would set off one of his headaches? She had been in a serene Bach chorale, floating, and the screams were like Stravinsky crashing in on her, splitting her. How could Ross be screaming?

He's in trouble, she thought. But what kind of—

The maniac. If he had gotten the name Laura from her purse, he had gotten her address, too. *I gave Ross to him,* she thought. It's not enough I have to be so negligent that Donny dies; I have to hand Ross to a maniac, too.

She flung herself off the cart, over a bluff on her left, and into the sand trap it sheltered. There was no mistaking the whining rip of a bullet going over her head or the magnified slapping report from the gun that shot it.

Ross was still yelling.

And it was at Janney the shot had been aimed.

So Ross, at least, was alive.

Sand was in her mouth and her eyes. She'd fallen trying to protect her cut hand and therefore came down so hard on her good hand that it, too, was trembling with pain.

Ross and I against a crazy with a rifle. Oh, God, you weren't kidding about the blind leading the blind, were you?

CHAPTER
TWELVE

KEVIN WAS TOTALLY SHOCKED by the sound of the man's voice. The tic in his cheek was leaping so frequently now that his jaw ached as if it had been propped open for a dentist. His head throbbed, and his nose hurt.

He struggled to keep his shock from interfering with his next shot. He continued to pull smoothly on the trigger, but his body had twitched when the man yelled and he was thrown off and had to compensate, and by the time his finger began to tighten for a second shot Laura was already falling. She'd taken the warning and jumped off the golf cart. He tried opening his eyes wider and then squinting in an effort to find her, focus on her, aim at her, but there was nothing in his scope. She was not on the ground, not in the cart, and not running.

Kevin swallowed and his mouth tasted bad and he was aware of being terribly thirsty.

A man. Who could it be? The house was empty. He'd checked all the bedrooms. The only room occupied upstairs was the one with the woman's clothing strewn all over the enormous bed. It was, of course, a bed for two. Was there a husband around?

He could not believe it. A man with the money to live in this house would have his own car and there was no car in the carport and no car had driven up Mashie Lane. And it was not a neighbor. There were only two houses

115

nearby, and both of them were obviously closed up for the season.

Some ten yards or more to the right of the empty golf cart he spotted the tip of what was probably an enormous sand trap. She's behind the bluff, Kevin thought. That's what happened before. Well, she's not getting away this time. The land slants up behind her, not down. She twitches an ankle and I'll see her. I'll shoot her joint by joint if I have to.

It was axiomatic to Kevin that a man was more of an enemy than a woman. He had to shoot down the woman, even though the only bad thing she represented was what she might say. With the man, Kevin had to worry about what he might *do*.

Man's not armed, thought Kevin, or he'd have shot me. He had plenty of time. So he's just outside, yelling a warning. I'll get him from one of the windows.

Kevin slid back toward the living room, from which direction the yell had seemed to come.

The two French doors were open, swinging very slightly.

But had the man come in or gone out?

For the first time in his entire life there was fear mixed into all Kevin's other emotions. It gave him a dark, smoking feeling, like dry ice, a chill so deep it burned him. If the man had left the house, it meant he'd previously been inside with Kevin, his presence completely unknown and unfelt.

Or had the man been outside all the time? Rocking on the porch perhaps? Waiting for his wife to come home from wherever she'd been. Were the doors open because the man had *come back in?* Was the man even now invisibly sharing space with Kevin? Crouching behind a door, waiting in a closet? Hunched behind a couch? Creeping upstairs to use a telephone extension?

Kevin had been out of the kitchen merely seconds, but when he paced back to check on Laura, there was a movement from the spot near the golf cart. He fired instantly through the open window slot.

He had never shot like that before. Blindly. Without

the slightest certainty of what he was aiming at. Kevin looked through the scope at the sand trap rim. Magnified four times, it remained a blur of night. There were so many trees and twigs in the way and it was so dark he could not even distinguish the cross hairs in the scope.

The man's voice vibrated in his memory: a strong baritone shout. All those trees and bushes in the backyard between Kevin and the sand trap behind which a man could stand. If Kevin were hit or attacked from behind, the rifle would do him little good.

All she has to do is lie there, thought Kevin, smoldering, and I can't get to her unless I expose myself to the man.

His left cheek shivered again, as if it were an animal's flank shaking off a fly.

I've got to go out there after her. I know exactly where she is. The way the land slants, she can't see me coming and she can't get away from me.

Two against one, thought Kevin. All right. If that's the way they want it, that's the way we'll play it. I can't see either of them, but I'll get them.

His fantasies about them were quite different. Laura he still wanted to kill with his hands, ripping her, but the man he wanted to shoot at a distance.

To watch Laura, he could not watch much else.

But the man would make a move. Men always did.

And Kevin would be ready.

Catherine Randallman saw the truck and recognized it: Grey's company truck, the liquid carrier.

Blew a tire? she thought. Ran out of fuel?

It was pointing at the oddest angle, into the woods, as if it had had to leave the road in desperation, to avoid an accident, perhaps.

She pulled onto the sandy shoulder and frowned at dark patches which stained the white sand. Leaving her headlights on, she got out of the car to inspect them. A nauseating stench rose from the sand.

What on earth? thought Catherine. Gagging, she ran to the cab of the truck, but it was empty.

Then they're both in Grey's car, she thought. They've both gone somewhere together.

I must trust Grey, she thought. Whatever he's doing, he's using good sense. And then she thought: But whatever Kevin's doing, he's using bad sense. Catherine swallowed against her fear and lifted the radiotelephone to call the village police.

This is like war, thought Janney. She was huddled under the overhang of the sand trap as she would huddle under a puff quilt on a January night. First World War, she thought. Trapped in the bunkers. The Germans had ritzy interior-decorated bunkers. I, Janney, am obviously an Englishman with a crummy shallow sand bunker.

Her hand was bleeding again, rhythmically, like a faint timpani roll. She tucked it under her opposite armpit and tightened her arm down hard. The pressure helped the pain. It even diminished the fear, channeling it down clenched arm muscles.

How could I have heard Ross yell from his room all the way out here? Janney thought. His room faces the front yard. I just don't think Ross could yell that loud. Maybe he's not in his bedroom. In his wheelchair then? In the kitchen? Living room? Screaming out opened windows? A prisoner of this man—or dead?

He couldn't be dead. Only one shot had been fired, and that was definitely at her. And this silence now, from the house, what did that mean? Was the crazy man looking for Ross?

She could think of no way and no place for Ross to hide.

I have to get up there and save him, she thought.

That merely entailed leaving the sand trap, crossing the grass, the rough, and the woods, going up the backyard and into the house. No big deal, in the moonlight, with a rifle's sights on her hiding place.

Two large blackbirds lit on the sand in front of her and stared. Carrion birds. Sizing me up? she wondered. She whisked her good hand at them, and reluctantly, with backward glances, they flew off.

Whatever she did, she'd need two hands, not one hand and a stub. Janney pulled the socks off her cut, and using teeth and right hand, tied the socks around her palm so her fingers would still be useful. All five still were. Whatever had been slashed was evidently not vital to finger working.

Ten fingers, Janney thought. Big deal. All a rifle needs is one.

The cut was aching so badly it felt as if her hand were going to self-amputate. God, she said irritably. And, crawling, put the cut on the tines of a sand rake. She cried out in pain and tucked her hand back up under her arm, rocking herself.

When the pain diminished, she kicked off one of her sneakers and poked the shaft of the rake into the sneaker toe. Holding the tines in her right hand, she raised the sneaker above the level of the bluff protecting her.

Even expecting it, she was not prepared for the instantaneous boom of the gun. She smacked against the sand, and the substance that had been so soft and yielding was like cement beneath her cheek. Janney spit out sand and examined the sneaker. He'd missed it, but then it was a very small target. Her body, her seven-pounds-overweight body, would not be so easy to miss.

She could place the crazy man all too well. He was considerably above her, which meant presumably in her house. But she could not place Ross at all.

There was no point in expecting somebody to hear the shots and come to investigate or call the police to do so. Holly Oak was a skeet shooting center, and in the woods beyond the golf courses there were active hunt clubs, taking pheasant, fox, deer, and duck in season. Near the clubs you could hear the arrhythmic bounce of tennis balls all day long; in the country, the sporadic crash of gunfire. It was night, but practice ranges were open in the evening, although not this late. There were no close neighbors to wonder about gunfire from the Fraser house.

Oh, God, help.

She put no exclamation point after her plea. It was more of a gulp. Help. A hiccup.

Useless, thought Janney, to ask God—or anyone else—for anything.

Ross had given away his position by yelling. Trying to move, his wheel rims glittering in the moonlight, would be suicidal. Obviously the guy had brought the rifle along to use. Ross tore off his bathrobe and draped it over the exposed side of the chair. Then he pulled as many of the bridal wreath branches as possible in front of his face.

The night was surprisingly noisy. The insects had not been the least disturbed by the sound of the gunfire. Ross found their racket annoying. It was even, somehow, triumphant, as if the cicadas had known perfectly well that their species would survive, no matter what happened to Ross and Janney.

Logically, now, the man would go out on the golf course to be sure he'd gotten Janney. Or would he head after Ross first, to finish him off?

Ross could not see the course. Sitting in the wheelchair, he was only three and a half feet tall. It occurred to Ross that the man had no way of knowing Ross was in a wheelchair. The man's eyes would be searching on his own level for the source of that shout.

Won't he be pleased when he finds out how little he's up against? thought Ross.

He was overwhelmed by his inability to deal with the man. We're losers, Janney and I, he thought. She's lost her baby, her husband, her marriage, her income, and her happiness. I've lost my legs, my strength, my health, my future, my mother, my brother, and my father. What a list. No wonder Avery left. How depressing to come home each day to a house that reeks of loss.

The night sounds began to separate in his mind. The air conditioner was still running and presumably would not shut off till October, set at sixty degrees like that. The golf cart was also running, though not moving.

And the house was silent.

I'm a good shot, thought Ross. The army trained me. If I had a rifle, too, it'd be different. But he had no weapon. Guns he could use; let the power of the gun do his work for him. Anything else would require strength from Ross. And he had none.

So Janney and I have to help each other. No neighbors. Nobody but me wondering why Janney's not home yet. The telephone inside, where the man is. The police unreachable. No way to hoist myself into a car, even if I had one to drive away. Anything resembling a weapon back indoors. Knives, hammers, screwdrivers — hammers, thought Ross. The tool shed.

Back when Avery still insisted that it was just a matter of attitude and Ross could be up and wheeling around, a mechanic here, a woodworker there, he'd fixed up a workshop for Ross. The tools were hung three feet off the ground.

And if the man indoors turned on the kitchen light, it would flood the adjacent carport and the tool shed that formed its side wall, and there he'd be, exposed in all his helplessness.

Cripple, thought Ross, goddamn cripple.

Hate ripped through him — not the usual apathy or self-pity, but hate, for being what he was.

There were heavy footsteps just inside the French doors. With a tremendous effort of will Ross did not turn to watch. His skin and eyes might catch the light. He told himself the green plaid bathrobe would look just like leaves in the dark.

In a moment the shoes tapped away from the door.

Ross took a breath so deep he sucked leaves in.

The rifle tip reappeared in the kitchen window.

Ross struggled with the why of the whole thing. Why would this man want to kill "Laura"? Why would he come at night, like a jungle sniper? Why would Janney appear by golf cart and react obediently and without question to Ross's command to get away? And why, having gotten them all in this position, would the man not come out of the house and finish them off? Why wait indoors?

But meditating was merely a way of postponing action,

a way of convincing himself he was doing something when he wasn't.

He wheeled himself around the front of the house while the man was occupied with the back. He was not sure what he would do with whatever he found in the tool shed. Ride with the tide, he told himself. A soldier works with what's available.

There was no padlock on the hasp of the tool shed. But Avery had locked everything. It had been one of their problems when he left: trying to break into their own rooms. Why wasn't the tool shed locked?

Because it was empty, that's why. He moved the tools to his basement, thought Ross. He gave up hoping I'd ever get out here and use them.

The shed held an old leaf broom, a car-washing bucket, sponges, a grass sprinkler, and a rusted flashlight.

Ross identified at last what he detested so thoroughly in the Gothic novels. Not the trembling girl. It was fine with Ross if beautiful girls hung around trembling. It was the hero. Always about thirty, rich, and strong. Always literally sweeping the girl off her feet. Active, thought Ross, staring into the shed. A Gothic hero can always act, not think.

Look upon this as an opportunity, Avery would have said. Here's your chance to fly, Ross! Come on, son! Chin up, think high, rise above this thing, don't let a mere war wound conquer you!

Right, Dad was right, Ross told himself. I can rise above it all. I can whip this guy with one wheel. It's all a matter of attitude.

Ross straightened up as if Avery's hand were pressing his spine. I'm a pilot, he told himself. I've got to get above the clouds. Rise beyond the storm. Use my brain, find my guts.

He lifted himself so much he pulled the armrests right off the wheelchair.

It's comical, thought Ross. It's truly funny. I'm a god-damned cripple out here in the carport trying to fly.

CHAPTER
THIRTEEN

ED FARLEY was a summer cop. Actually he worked winters, too, but in local parlance, a summer cop was the guy who directed traffic, wore a uniform, and typed up camping permits. Ed had never been to a police academy, although he had spent two mornings sort of learning how to use the gun strapped to his waist. The instructor said the only rules that really mattered were: (a) keep the holster closed so kids couldn't extract the gun, and (b) don't use it.

Ed Farley followed these rules precisely and had long forgotten the minor details of how to aim and shoot the thing. Unlike the other members of the force (if, as the locals said, you could exaggerate and call them forceful), he was not a hunter and had no guns of his own. That's okay, said Bob Shearing, who was his superior in years, if not brains, we need a pacifist on the force, makes us look good on the hire-the-hard-core-unemployed lists.

Catherine Randallman stood very still watching him. She had been standing very still for many minutes, waiting for Ed to get here, and she had a sensation she might need to stand still forever, keeping a grip on time and her thoughts, keeping Grey safe by not allowing the future to come.

She and Ed had determined that there were two dark mixtures on the ground: orangy black stuff that stank with

123

the same odor as the truck and dark, sticky stuff that was blood.

Ed used the radio in his car to call the other policeman. She listened to his soft, almost unbelievably thick accent drawling out the situation. "Deer's bin here a awr er two, Ah think...lossa bluyd...don' know...Mizrus Randall-man say her man been gone a awr er two, too. Kinda matches, yer think so?"

No, no, don't let it match, thought Catherine. She had spent her life going through thick and thin with Grey, the entire marriage ceremony, the richer, the poorer, the sickness, the health, the better, the worse. This was the payoff: retirement, the good years, the marriage wrapped in decades of understanding each other.

Kevin, she told herself. It's Kevin's blood. Maybe Grey took Kevin to a hospital for some sort of emergency.

But even as she tottered toward Ed to tell him to call the hospitals about that, she knew that Kevin would be the bloodletter, not the bleeding.

Fourth of July, thought Grey. They really raised money for fireworks this year, didn't they?

He could not see the glittering sky. Could not see anything.

I am alive, thought Grey.

Perhaps because rifles were meant for distance, not close work. Perhaps the spray of blood had convinced Kevin of Grey's death, and he had not explored, as Grey's hand did now, the shoulder where the bullet had actually penetrated.

Alive, but by a hairsbreadth.

Trunk of a car, thought Grey. His own, he supposed. The trunk lacked the luxurious comfort of the other interior areas of the Cadillac. The trunk, in fact, was downright painful.

Kevin. My nephew. Shot me. Meant to kill me. Enjoyed it.

Grey lay quietly, helplessly, his knees bent into protruding metal, his skull resting on a bolt. It was not the

Fourth of July. Kevin was shooting at something. At someone, more likely.

My God, thought Grey, where did we go wrong with
him? Environment. That's me and my sister and our families. We surrounded Kevin.

Did we create this?

For a moment Kevin thought Laura must be planning
a yard sale and was storing her junk in the dining room.
There was a path around the room, but it led past a bed,
not a table, and the clutter of the room was astonishing.
The ceiling was crisscrossed with ropes, and the shelves
slid when his fingers brushed them. The bed was covered
with trays and boxes.

If Laura knew he was in a front room, she might have
guts enough to run during her few seconds of safety. He
did not dare turn on the lights to examine the room. But
in the dark he could not analyze it, and he did not even
want to walk around the bed. In a room like this the man
with the voice would have no trouble hiding.

Kevin dropped to his knees so his silhouette would not
show in the window and reached up to turn on the light.
The lights blinded him to the outdoors, but he did not
intend to have them on for more than a second or two. He
took one good look at the dining room.

It was an invalid's bedroom. A hospital bed with a rail
around it. Piles of books and magazines. Binoculars, pen-
cils, crosswords, a small Sony television.

A sick guy, thought Kevin, almost laughing in relief.
Probably falls out of bed when he rolls over. Bedroom in
the dining room because he can't get upstairs.

Contemptuously Kevin turned off the lights and returned to the kitchen window. Laura would not have had
enough time to move during any of these explorations to
try to find the owner of the voice. Invalid, he thought
dismissively. What am I worried about? I'll go out after
Laura right now. Kill her, forget about the man, take off.
I'm running out of time. Aunt Catherine has probably

called the police nine times by now because Grey wasn't there for their precious eleven o'clock news.

He put his left hand on the back door knob, and the boxes on the invalid's bed registered in his brain as a ham radio transmitter, a CB set, and a telephone.

In twenty years of playing organ in all denominations of churches and a number of temples, Janney had found that certain congregations shared a basic ceremonial belief: Silence was evil.

Every instant a preacher was not speaking or a choir not singing, the organist was expected to provide "traveling music" to fill the dreaded quiet moments. More often than not, "silent" prayer was a time for Janney to diddle on the keyboard while the minister timed the congregation for forty-five seconds of meditation (apparently the maximum time ministers felt their flocks could spend in thought). Janney detested traveling music. She generally used phrases of Bach and other baroque composers instead of relying on her own poor improvisatory ability, and earnest parishioners often came up to tell her what cute little melodies she composed and how she ought to try to get them published sometime.

The silence from her house was thicker than anything she had ever experienced in a church. It reverberated with unshot bullets and unbroken bones. It waited.

For what? Oh, God, for what? Janney thought.

Mentally she apologized to all the Methodists she'd castigated for not allowing silence in their services.

They were right.

In silence you were forced to think.

Kevin clung to his rifle as if the gun were fastened to something solid and would be able to pull him out of his troubles. His palms dripped with perspiration and the rifle slid dangerously out of his grip, and when he held it tighter, it slid faster. He wiped his palms on his shorts and used the quilted place mat to dry the rifle.

No, he told himself, and emphasized the negative by

saying it aloud. "No." The guy had not called anybody. Kevin had, after all, slipped noiselessly into the house and stood in the living room, getting his breath, listening, deciding if the house was empty or if Laura had a husband upstairs asleep. He'd tiptoed up, come right down, and sat silently in the kitchen. If a finger had moved a dial or tapped out a message or opened up a CB channel, he'd have heard.

It's okay, Kevin thought. He pressed the rifle against his trembling cheek, like a hot-water bottle, soothing himself.

The house seemed to be crawling with unseen men and shifting shadows. It was less a duck blind from which to shoot Laura than a trap in which to be caught himself. Kevin walked out the kitchen door and onto the narrow back porch. There was one chair on the porch, just one. But two people living here.

Kevin bent, listening again. He could go through the backyard, and the woods, and over the rough in one minute. But the yard was full of thick shrubbery, laced over with fat limbs of leafy trees, dotted with gardens and railroad ties and small sagging fences.

Maybe the sick guy was walking for help. Had been walking ever since he screamed at Laura. Maybe he didn't need the equipment in his bedroom. Was on his way to use someone else's.

Hell with it, thought Kevin. I'll kill Laura and run. Get to that Yamaha motorcycle place other side of number five. Dirt roads, hunting grounds, riding trails. They'll never find me. I'll be out of the state by dawn.

He left the porch to go finish Laura off.

Bob Shearing liked being a cop in Holly Oak. His job was nothing like police work shown on television or in books or even in Associated Press reports of crime across America. Bob had no experience with much of anything in comparison to those police. Holly Oak had never had a riot or a strike or a gang or a mob. It rarely had robberies because each inn or condo had its own security people. Bob directed traffic, told visitors where to cash travelers' checks, drove drunk visitors to their hotels, and called ambulances when the drunk visitors tried to get home without his help. He patrolled the houses of wealthy visitors currently visiting elsewhere and chatted with the storekeepers in the village about how life wasn't what it used to be.

Rather like Holly Oak, his tasks were placid and pleasant.

Bob Shearing was a cop steeped in optimism rather than cynicism, which, of course, was the sort that the Holly Oak atmosphere required. Whenever Bob gave talks to schoolchildren about never taking rides with strangers (the fact that small kids lived in Holly Oak was more startling than the idea of kidnappers thereof), not once did it cross his mind that one day he himself might have to tangle with such a stranger. "Actually," said Mrs. Randallman, in a voice faded like an old sheet, "Kevin Clary, our nephew, called this evening from the truck and said things had gone wrong and would I get Grey for him."

Kevin Clary.

Bob realized that he did, after all, know someone in the stranger category.

Janney had turned up a pine cone in the sand. It was still green and firm, its little shingled sides wrapped tightly around its invisible core. Janney stroked it.

There were far fewer evergreens up Boston way than in North Carolina. Winter in Boston was unremittingly gray and dreary, black silhouettes of gaunt trees against a faded sky, dirty slush thrown up by passing cars on vulnerable ankles. Yet her memories of Boston were woven of concerts and friends and laughter and love.

Boston, she thought.

It had the sound of home. What, after all, did Holly Oak mean to her?

I could be like Avery. Turn around and go.

Why hadn't he told her he felt like fleeing? Why hadn't she told him she felt that way, too? Why had they talked about the price of gasoline and the chances of rain when they could have been talking about running away? He had not even taken a toothbrush. He'd just left. What a good idea, Janney thought. I'm ready. When does my plane leave?

I've had it with my problems, God. I'm going off into another world where skies are blue and hopes are high and futures are good. Who needs this crummy scene with crippled stepsons, lousy jobs, dead children, and deserting husbands? That's not what I had in mind when I left the conservatory. I would have submitted a list to you, God, but I thought you knew I wanted everything to work out happily ever after.

She peeked up behind the golf cart to see if she could leave.

The maniac was on her back porch, hunched over in the listening position peculiar to timpanists tuning during a flute solo.

Janney threw her pine cone across the sand. It was about as satisfying as slamming a paper door.

She was not going to be able to rearrange her life. Very probably she was not going to have a life to rearrange.

"Fifty-six years old, five-eight, one seventy-five, gray hair, gray eyes, bifocals. Wearing a navy plaid sports jacket and khaki pants."

It sounded old, dull, and dumpy. It was not, could not be, Grey that Shearing was describing.

The blood in front of Catherine was like a brown crust on the bread of white sand.

"A 'fifty-seven Cadillac Eldorado. Real museum piece. Stainless steel roof, red exterior, fins sticking about six feet behind the wheels, great big bullet-shaped chrome bumper. You can't miss it."

He was making the car sound like a joke. Of course, in a way, it was. No one could help laughing at what they all had aspired to a few decades earlier. But Grey would never abandon his metal baby. There was no joke about that.

Bob finished transmitting to the state police. The three

of them looked at the truck, the spilled, stinking dark liquid, the blood, and the deer. "A truck gets stuck in the sand," said Bob. "But why wouldn't they just wait until morning and get a tow?"

"Has sumpin' tu do with th' deer," said Ed. "Kevin don' have no lahsince, yew know, sence he keeled Rory."

"But he wouldn't call Grey about the deer," objected Catherine. "Grey's the last person Kevin would want around if he were hunting illegally."

"Where would they have been headed on a Saturday night with a truck full of dye?" Bob asked her.

"Is it dye? I thought it was fuel."

"Don't rightly know," said Bob.

Sickness rose in Catherine's throat. Some of Kevin did stick to us, she thought. Or deep down, did we infect Kevin with our well-hidden evil? "Grey has some property up in Randolph County," she said softly. She and Grey had never discussed the purpose of that land. Yet somehow she knew. And knew, too, that it was wrong and that she and Grey were equally culpable. "He carries trash up there to dump," she said, and then she forced herself to say it correctly, "carries liquid wastes." Bob was staring at her, confused. In the shadows cast by the car headlights and his own powerful flashlight he looked very dumb. His jaw seemed to hang down to his sharp Adam's apple. "Grey said something last week about having to drive up there soon," Catherine added.

Bob moved his jaw, as if, cowlike, he had to chew cud in order to think. "You mean poisons?" he said at last.

"I don't *know* that there are poisons in it," said Catherine. But I do know, she thought. Oh, God, what have we done? "I just know it's leftovers Grey doesn't keep permanently around the plant."

"Where is this property?" said Bob Shearing.

"I couldn't find it by night. It isn't marked. It's up past Harsh Creek Road, where it intersects at Deep River and runs into West Sunrise."

"West Sunrise?" said Ed.

Bob snickered. "Sure," he said. "'Cause you're west of the sun when it rises."

"But," said Catherine Randallman, "why head there? They're in the Cadillac now. There's nothing for them to go up to Randolph County *for*. Why not drive home, drop Kevin off, and deal with this mess in the morning?"

Bob chewed, whether air or tobacco or his own tongue, she could not tell. "Well, ma'am," said Bob Shearing, drawling like Ed, "mebbe either Grey or Kevin has something else to dump now."

CHAPTER

FOURTEEN

Ross PUT THE BRAKE ON HIS CHAIR, leaned forward, gripping the door to keep himself from falling out, and grabbed the flashlight. When he had it, he could not get himself upright again. He folded over, panting, and the headache became an invasive cancer that was going to tumble him right out of the chair.

He felt as if he were being ironed.

At any other time, in pain as severe as this, he'd have been flat in bed, not wanting so much as the pressure of a thin blanket over him.

Grit your teeth, son, Avery would cry, like a cheerleader to a losing team. Ross had always half expected his father to start doing jumping jacks—anything to raise a little enthusiasm. What's a little pain, Ross? Do it anyway.

As quickly as he could move his aching wrists, he pulled the chair back across the front of the house and into the thick shrubbery that separated the Fraser property from the Schmidts'. Donny had often done a little judicious pruning of lower branches to make passages for himself, but Donny had been much smaller and slimmer than Ross and the wheelchair. Ross grabbed branches and twisted them out of his wheel spokes, tugging himself ahead without getting caught in the vines, keeping his head ducked painfully low. When the wheels sank in a soft, sandy place, he had to haul himself forward by hanging onto the bushes. He thought he would probably pull himself onto the ground and leave the wheelchair standing immobile in the sand, but it moved with him, and then he was facing an impenetrable patch of firethorn that Donny had been able to scoot beneath and for Ross was an unlockable gate.

Still, the Schmidts' house, built close to the lot line, was no more than thirty feet away. The window nearest him was roughly twice as high as his reach. The Schmidts had a burglar alarm connected to the police department. Every window was wired. He could not get to a phone, but he could still call the police.

Ross panted just holding the flashlight. There was no way he could toss the flashlight one-handed like a baseball pitcher. He'd have to throw with both hands. Basketball hoop, he told himself, staring at the blank pale rectangle of the window. He could make out the ball fringe on Mrs. Schmidt's curtains. Flying, he thought derisively. Sure, Avery. For me they'll have to spread foam on the runway.

Ross aimed for the window, heaved the flashlight with all his remaining strength, and after a mild tap against the house wall, it tumbled with a faint crackle into the mulch around the azalea bed.

The rage that shivered through him was impotent. For the first time in years he had had a chance to *do* something, and there was nothing he could do.

He strained his eyes, trying to see another object to throw: a stick, a broken brick, an old golf ball. But there was nothing. The Schmidts' yard was as clean as a vacuumed carpet.

He would have to get back in his own house and use that phone. Ross turned the wheelchair around with difficulty and began hauling himself out of the shrubbery.

The man with the rifle appeared on the back porch.

Ross ceased to move or breathe.

If I just sit and wait, dawn will eventually come. Sunshine. Things always look better in the morning. That's Janney's theory anyhow. But that presupposes that your problems go away during the night. And what if this character doesn't go away? Then what?

Then by day he can see each of us perfectly. No strip of leaves is going to protect me from a bullet after the sun comes up.

Pain swept up him, forcing him to bend over, close his eyes, swallow against it.

I'm flying, Ross told himself. Mentally he pulled handles, turned dials, set gauges, thought high thoughts, envisioned the sky above him and the land dropping away below him.

He did not get above the pain. Land and try again, thought Ross.

The man on the back porch was listening to something. His body was slightly arched, as if he could hear with his flesh as well as with his ears. Slowly, carefully, as if treading on quicksand, the man walked down the ramp and into the backyard. Skirting the fat hydrangeas, he headed for Janney and the golf course.

Ross hurt so much he could not even watch. God damn this pain, he screamed at God. I won't have it, I won't!

The guy had left both the living room and the kitchen doors open. Ross had to find the strength to get in the house. And what a help that will be to Janney, he thought. When he'll have killed her before I can even get to the goddamned ramp.

The left wheel of his chair crackled noisily on some dead magnolia leaves, and the rifleman turned, dropped to one knee, and aimed directly at him.

Sunday golfers started early, especially in summer. The manager of the Halfway House at course number three slammed the alarm clock button down before it went off and staggered into the bathroom to slosh cold water over his face. It was a detestable routine, but any variation and he'd find himself drifting right back to sleep.

Sunday, for reasons known only to a sadistic club president, the Halfway House had to serve breakfast. Bick felt cold toast and congealed sausage rounds were all that dawn golfers deserved, but no, it had to be ham biscuits, pan-cakes, toast, eggs, bacon, sausage, grits, applesauce, or-ange juice, you name it. And his cook tended to go back to sleep after slamming her alarm clock off. It was Ellen's belief that civilized people should have brunch, not break-fast, and she had come to Holly Oak thinking that only civilized people would be there, so she saw no reason to exert herself for the barbarians who demanded English muffins in the wee hours on a day of rest.

Bick found his clothes, checked groggily under the flu-orescent stove light to be sure his socks matched, and headed for his car. Still dark out. But all over Holly Oak visitors were actually thrilling to the sound of their alarm clocks, eagerly swinging their feet off the mattresses, thinking of the good hot breakfast Bick would be serving at the ninth hole. Most of them would actually drive to the Halfway House first and then drive back to start at the first tee. There was no trusting people to behave de-cently.

At this hour he even drove sluggishly.

Bick parked in his favorite space, slightly below and quite far from the Halfway House, where his car would be in shade all day long and he wouldn't burn his fingers on the door handle when he had a chance to leave in the afternoon. Yawning, Bick walked over the parking lot and threaded through the shrubs (only in Holly Oak was it deemed necessary to turn every fourth parking slot over to a miniark of shrubs and trees) to the pavilion entrance.

He was feeling for the key in his pocket when he saw the broken glass and the gaping black holes in the mul-tipaned window.

He was afraid.

Kevin was horribly, permeatingly afraid. He could smell himself. He did not know which of them he hated more: Laura for breaking his nose or the man for frightening him.

The sound had been behind him. When he faced it, he could feel Laura, safe somewhere, slithering belly down

out of her sand trap, laughing at him, knowing that Kevin
Clary was afraid of some sick wimp. Laugh at me, thought
Kevin grimly. We'll see how you laugh with a bullet be-
tween your eyes.

God, thought Ross incredulously, you did damn the pain.

The pain was below him, the dizziness at his feet. It
was like taking an elevator to the floor above. Hey, Dad,
thought Ross, you were right. My plane just came in.

The man lifted his rifle and aimed it roughly at Ross,
though somewhat higher and to the right.

I get my plane in the air and some saboteur puts a bomb
on it, thought Ross. If that isn't just like life.

The man moved slowly, swingingly, facing first Ross
and the shrubbery, then Janney and her sand trap. It took
Ross some moments to grasp that the man with a rifle was
afraid of him. Afraid of the anonymous crackle of leaves
in a dark unknown wood.

As long as I'm silent, he'll get calmer. In a moment he'll
go after Janney after all. And what do I do? If I yell at Janney, there's nowhere she can go and nothing she can do. If
I yell, he'll fire at me, and that won't help Janney either.
But I can't move without noise, so I can't get into the house
to use the phone. And even if I get in and call the cops, by
then he'll have killed Janney twice and driven away.

Ross glanced up his driveway. Half on Mashie Lane,
half in the drive was a huge dark car that seemed to have
a fishpond for a roof.

The moon drifted behind a cloud. Ross could no longer
see much of the man or what he was doing with the rifle.
Maybe I should just talk to him. Introduce myself. Ask
him if he's really looking for a Laura. If maybe he's got
the wrong cul-de-sac here.

It seemed like a good way to get a bullet in the lungs.
But it was his lungs or Janney's. An hour ago he had been
lying on his mattress yearning to do something for his
stepmother. Never ask for anything, Ross thought. You
might get it.

He hauled himself forward over the crackling leaves.

*   *   *

Personally Janney felt half the standing ovations she'd ever witnessed came from audiences so glad to stand up at last they didn't care what cultural price they paid. Her entire body was throbbing from keeping the awkward hunch beneath the grassy bluff that protected her sand trap. The cut in her hand was getting hot and feverish.

Back in her abortive violin stage (she'd never got the hang of the required vibrato) Janney had sat through long, long concerts, waiting her turn to throw in a few notes. And she had sat on organ benches, through long sermons, long laymen's reports, long Sunday school award programs. But never, never had she sat through anything as long as this. I could lie down, she thought. That would be more comfortable. But it seemed ridiculously improper to stretch out as if sunbathing when she might be shot at any moment.

It's been all of three or four minutes, she told herself. I just have to keep calm. But *why* is this man after me? A car theft? Who even cares? How would I have known he was stealing anything, anyway?

She was crying. It was the identical weeping that had begun shortly after Donny's death, the week it became obvious that Avery was not returning and she would have to stagger on alone. Tears simply poured out of her eyes. She did not whimper, sniffle, or sob but only supplied the eyes and the cheeks down which the tears rolled.

That man's got the patience of a born-again proselytizer, Janney thought. He'll wait all night for me to flinch, and then he'll get me. No wonder they call this a sand trap. I have to sit here and be even more patient than he could ever be. I have to—

It occurred to Janney that the man was not necessarily bound to stay in her house to do his shooting. If he left the house (and what could stop him? Certainly not Ross), he could stroll up to her sand trap and kill her as easily as he could a caged animal.

She was amazed at how quickly an idea came to her.

The golf cart was still humming. How long would the battery last? Would it die just when she needed it? Janney crawled down the sandpit to where she'd flung herself off the golf cart. It had stopped when her foot left the accelerator, but with the key still turned, the motor had continued to run.

The sand trap was very long, curving, with a dip at each end. Just crawling in it proved that the sand was too deep for running. As long as she was in the sand, she'd stagger. To move fast, she had to be out on the grass.

Janney took off her necklace. It was a leather thong with five fat ceramic beads strung on it. Letting the beads slide off into the sand, she maneuvered herself directly behind the raised seat part of the golf cart. For the second time she slowly raised the sneaker on the plastic rake handle. There was no shot. She waved it gently. No shot then either. Did that mean he couldn't see behind the cart or that he knew it was a sneaker and wasn't about to fall for the same trick twice?

She set the sand rake down. Taking the leather thong in her hand, she began slowly and cautiously raising her head over the rim of the bluff. How unfortunate that her eyes were housed in the same appendage as her brain. If she could stick up her elbow and look around with that, it would be a far less frightening maneuver.

No bullet ripped through her skull. Probably she would never know if he did shoot her. Only know if he did not. How reassuring.

Janney reckoned conservatively that she had heard a thousand sermons. She now realized that none of them had addressed real problems. Like, do you risk having your brain divided on the off chance your stepson is still alive and you might—under the circumstances that was almost a laugh cue—save him?

Do you always have to try? she thought. Whatever happened to the good old theory of surrender?

But if she had tried harder with Donny, run faster after him, screamed louder at the driver of the car, lectured Donny daily about the dangers of the road, he would be alive now. How tedious that life always required the utmost of you. Why could life not consist of lazing around a pool exempt from mosquitoes and sunburn?

The moonlight disappeared behind a cloud. Darkness. Blessed darkness. She remembered waiting in her car at a red light with Donny impatient in his car seat. Saying to him, "Blow it out, Donny," and his crow of glee when, sure enough, he blew the stoplight green. Had coincidence blown out the moon? Or God?

Janney crawled over three feet of grass to the cart. With stiff fingers she knotted the end of the thong around the narrow metal rod that supported the fringed canopy and pierced the floor next to the accelerator. There was neither sound nor light from the house. Very likely the maniac was busy training the sights of his rifle on her hair.

She looped the thong around the accelerator and saw that her original idea would not quite work. The instant she began tying down the accelerator, the cart would begin moving and she'd be unable to complete the knots that would keep it moving.

She paused. It was like an orchestral production that really, intensely mattered. When every ounce of musical skill was being summoned, the combined tensions of finger and arm and leg muscles resulted, one hoped, in a superlative performance. Janney's whole body seemed to be waiting for some vital cue.

She could not move her fingers to the key.

Perhaps because the only conductor of this performance was chance.

Janney's face was bent over her wrists, and her hands were drenched by her tears. A wet thong will make a tighter knot, she told herself. She turned the motor off, hoping the man would not instantly register the lack of sound, tied the accelerator down, and flicked the key back to start.

The cart began trundling forward. Janney rolled backward into the sand trap again, landing, inevitably, on the sand rake. She scuttled down the opposite length of the sandpit. The moving golf cart was not attracting the man's attention. She had expected him to shoot at it.

Oh, God, he knows perfectly well what I'm up to. Or he's standing right here already, waiting for me to pop up.

There was no time to waste deliberating. The cart was getting to its turn in the path. When the blacktop curved, the cart would not. It would tumble into the sand trap, and her little trick would be obvious. He's watching the cart, she told herself. My end of the sand is safe.

The instant that Ross pulled himself out of the shelter of the shrubbery, disregarding the crunch of leaves and the breaking of twigs, the man with the rifle moved on into the narrow strip of woods, making enough crackle himself that he didn't hear Ross, and strode purposefully through the trees toward Janney.

It was like the moment of Donny's death, when Ross had been unable to do anything but sit and scream. All these months later he could still throb with the agony of not having been able to save Donny. I'm not doing it again, Ross thought. I'm not sitting here *again*, waiting while someone gets killed.

He hauled the wheelchair forward to the blacktop path, panting, frantic, with a sense that if he could just move, he could accomplish things. Once on the path he rolled speedily down the gentle curves toward the wood. The man with the rifle emerged from the wood onto the rough just as Ross coasted into the trees behind him. And at the same moment the golf cart began to move.

It moved by itself. Eerily, impossibly, as if powered by Janney's ghost.

The man with the rifle stopped short, staring, lifting his rifle but doing it uncertainly, more to protect himself than to attack. Ross did not slow down. The speed, the breeze fanning his face, the sense of strength reminded Ross of being sixteen and having his driver's license for the first time: flooring the accelerator and feeling tough and invincible.

Tough, no. Invincible, no. Accelerating, yes. For one wild moment Ross thought he would be able to crash into the man with enough force to knock him over. Snatch the rifle. With the rifle, he, Ross, could run this crazy show.

But the man was not standing on the blacktop, and if Ross tried to turn himself onto the grass, he'd merely flip the wheelchair.

I forgot to ask myself what I planned to do when I caught up to the guy, thought Ross. I might as well be hurtling off a cliff.

The golf cart purred to itself, moving on down the course as if it had better things to do than hang around.

Suddenly Janney burst out of the sandpit.

CHAPTER

FIFTEEN

"WELL, MRS. RANDALLMAN," said Bob Shearing, "we'll get right on it. Ed here will drive behind you and take you and your Buick home, and I'll—"

"Home? I don't want to go home. I want to go with you and find out what's happening!" They regarded her gently and escorted her to the Buick. For the first time in her life Catherine felt a spurt of the rage of women's liberation. How dare these two fools send her home while they, who didn't even know Grey, searched for him?

"Mrs. Randallman, what if nothing is wrong after all, and ten minutes from now your husband pulls into the driveway? Or telephones to ask you to pick him up somewhere? You have to be there to answer the phone."

That's the trouble with arguments, thought Catherine. There are always two sides to them. Why am I not the sort of woman who can stand steadfastly on one side? Why am I always scurrying around seeing everybody else's angles? They opened the door to her Buick. Catherine thought: No. I've taken a side and I'm keeping it. If Grey were going to telephone or appear, he'd have done it hours ago. "I can't possibly drive," she said. "I'm too shaky."

The two policemen looked at her irritably. She returned their looks as blandly as she could. "Yes, ma'am," said Ed with a sigh. They locked up the Buick and deposited Catherine in the Volkswagen Rabbit that Bob drove. Ed had a Volkswagen Beetle.

"You like these for police cars?" she said to Bob Shearing.

He seemed to have to think about that. "They turn around easily," he said. "They get good mileage. They're better built than any American car I've ever used."

"And they're cute," said Catherine. "That's what matters around here, you know. Being cute." She could hear a bitterness in her voice that seemed to have no source and no reason. Shearing looked at her in surprise and mumbled something about preferring a little more legroom, that was all.

The police radio crackled like bacon.

There had been a break-in at one of the Halfway Houses. "Some stupid kid his first time trying to rob someplace," said Shearing irritably. "There's no money there. Nothing valuable around unless you're prison-term desperate for a dozen golf balls." He listened to the report. "Tell 'em it'll have to wait."

They passed the Community Church. A car Bob recognized immediately as Mrs. Fraser's was in its driveway. Her worthless husband had had a special paint job done on it. A policeman became quickly acquainted with a town's odd personalities, a slot for which Mrs. Fraser had qualified a year or so ago. He doubted that she knew him, but Bob was familiar with her midnight route home from the shopping mall because the patrol car often saw her. On Saturday mornings, when she went into the grocery store with a list that seemed to overwhelm her and glazed eyes that seemed unable to decipher it, she always parked crooked. Bob never ticketed her because of the little boy he had helped scrape up off the road.

Car finally broke down, thought Bob, feeling sorry for the woman. He said into his radio, "Telephone Frasers' place, will you? Mashie Lane. See if Mrs. Fraser got home all right."

Grey discovered the reason he had not yet suffocated. Kevin, in his haste, had not slammed the trunk down hard enough for it to latch completely. Grey began to work at the gap, trying to manipulate it all the way open.

I could call Kevin, he thought, listening to the gunfire. Tell him, it's okay, you didn't kill me. We'll tell everyone it was an accident, don't worry about it.

Kevin would not worry about it. He would just finish the job.

Grey could beg for a doctor forever and—no, not forever. Kevin wouldn't listen to him for one minute. Rory had not died immediately—they could tell from the amount of blood he had lost—and Kevin had not gone to a doctor.

Grey slid into a hideous evil dream, half conscious, half not, in which Rory died while Kevin giggled and old fat collie dogs slobbered over Grey's shoulder and fireworks exploded.

The pain reminded him of the story of the little boy from Sparta who let the fox eat out his belly. There was a fox eating Grey at the same time that Rory and the collie swam through him.

He had his fingers stuck in a metal trap. Foxes and fingers were biting him.

No, he was trying to open the lid. He was in his own car, he was trying to get out; the metal was a latch, a simple latch; he had to retain his ability to think, he could not fall apart into these terrifying dreams.

The latch opened, and the trunk bobbed up, far beyond Grey's reach, like a vast lid on a can of pain-filled worms.

He saw stars and trees, and he thought: Kevin will be back soon. And when he comes, he'll see I'm still alive, and he'll finish the job that is my death.

In Kevin there would be no pity and no remorse.

Grey wondered if nature had equipped Kevin that way. If Kevin was possibly too primitive, too much a throwback, for emotions like compassion and sorrow.

He scrabbled at the rim of the deep trunk like an animal trying to get out of a trap.

* * *

The two police cars entered the village proper. At this hour it was deserted and quiet. A few streetlamps cast a gentle glow over the shuttered shops. It looked British and civilized. It was impossible to go on imagining that Grey, her Grey, fresh from a symphony board meeting, had been murdered by the side of the road. All that blood belonged to the deer, she told herself, dismissing the fact that many yards had separated the deer and the blood.

"Bob?" said the dispatcher. The voice splintered like thin china on a tile floor. She could barely understand. "Yeah?" said Bob Shearing. He signaled a left. Ed followed them like a lamb. If there was one thing Ed was good at, it was following.

"Nobody answered at the Fraser place."

"There's always somebody home at Frasers'. The older son is war-injured and never goes out. You sure you called the right number?"

"I toll ya. There's nobody home."

His words were so distorted, Catherine felt like a decoder.

"Something else," said the splinters.

"Yeah?"

"The guy from the Halfway House called back. He's searched the place with some staff that came in early. There's blood all over the men's room and a wallet belonging to Kevin Clary."

After all his preparation Kevin wasn't ready for her presence, didn't have his rifle up, and couldn't fire. Kevin grabbed at her, and she screamed a huge, thick, terrified scream and lurched away from him. Kevin wheeled to shoot her as she fled, and there between him and Laura was a wheelchair.

Kevin stared at it.

It reflected in the moonlight. A hunched-over cripple sat in it, head twisted as if the cranium were too heavy for the cripple to keep erect. Laura, incredibly, did not go on running but stopped almost instantly to stand beside the wheelchair.

For perhaps two or three seconds action was beyond
Kevin. Just as he had not been able to grasp the misshapen
objects in the room behind the church organ, he was not
quite able to grasp who and why this pair of people were
motionlessly, silently facing him.

Only the rifle seemed real to Kevin. He was entirely
disoriented. He could scarcely remember how he had ever
gotten to this spot or what he had expected to accomplish
here anyway.

Shit, how unobservant, he thought. Normal people don't
need ramps. I walked down that ramp at the house and
never even wondered about it. This is the voice that yelled
to her. The invalid.

Kevin despised illness. He never even liked to think
about it, let alone associate with it. And between him and
Laura, who had won every round so far, hit him and hurt
him and broken his nose, and forced him to waste hours
when he should have been moving along, was a cripple.

Wheelchair, thought Kevin, suddenly almost nauseated. What if the man didn't have any legs? If there was
anything worse than illness, it was deformity. With an
effort Kevin lowered his gaze. Yes, legs. Flimsy little pale
bedroom slippers hanging limply on skinny white ankles.

I was afraid of that? thought Kevin.

From the road came the sounds of traffic. The end of
night. Christ, he had to get moving. He stepped forward
to shove the wheelchair out of his way so he could reach
Laura. He had things to show her. A woman, a goddamned
woman his mother's age or something, decrepit, a church
organist, of all feeble occupations, and she'd hurt him.

Kevin grinned at her.

They were taking corners without slowing down, Bob
yelling into the radio. Catherine clung to the door handle
and the seat belt. Bob had come to conclusions she could
not follow and was driving at a speed she thought insane.
But if Bob was right about Kevin and these poor Fraser
people, insanity was endemic tonight.

They raced back up Deep River Road, down through

the maze of spur roads that decorated it, onto the long curve that was Mashie Lane.

Toward the end of the road, a curving shine that could only be the metallic roof of Grey's Cadillac was visible.

Catherine was out of the police car and running toward it before Bob, and Ed trailing along after them, had even come to a stop. She did not need daylight to know the Caddy. Even in the dark it reeked of conspicuous consumption and ostentatious gadgetry.

The trunk of the car was resting open, the lid bobbing slightly in the breeze. Except that there was no breeze. The air was hot and still.

Catherine stopped running. The two Volkswagens stopped moving. Ed and Bob got out.

The lid waved like Pandora's box, about to empty itself of evil. A pair of eyes looked out at Catherine.

She screamed, and her scream echoed back at her from the golf course, and then Ed and Bob were screaming, too, but at a distance. She could not imagine where they had gone.

It was her husband, it was Grey, all bulging eyes and groping fingers, a caricature of himself, reaching for her like a spider. She stifled another scream, but it came anyway, from someone else's throat. "Grey?" whispered Catherine, lifting the hood higher. He seemed unable to talk, and his gestures were as uninterpretable as if he were a deaf person using Cyrillic letters. Catherine's hands were so wet they slid off the hood. When she reached in to help him, she found him enveloped by a damp, crusty mess, as if he had come down with leprosy or started leaking. His fingers grazed her cheek. Catherine jerked back from their gritty texture, hitting her head on the lock mechanism of the raised hood. She tried to call the two policemen to help her. She could not imagine why they were not with her, lifting, assisting, comforting. She could not remember their names to ask them to come, and she found herself like her husband, mute and confined to useless gestures.

"Kevin!" said one of the cops loudly. "Kevin, what the hell are you up to?"

Grey's fingers scrabbled around her neck. The texture of his hands was like something out of a horror movie. She was reminded of a play she had been in many, many years ago: *The Monkey's Paw*. The parents are given three wishes from the dried magic paw, and they wish to have their son, mangled to death by machinery, return to life. And he does return. Mangled.

Grey's hands were like the dried, shriveled evil monkey's paw.

She heard the cops running away, toward the house, and felt overpoweringly confused. What was the matter with them? Why weren't they calling the ambulance or helping Grey out of the trunk?

"Kevin?" they yelled. "Hey, Kevin!"

Janney had never in her life seen anything as terrifying as the satisfaction in the man's eyes when he focused on her. She felt more like a meal than a woman. If the crazy man had licked his lips, she would not have been surprised. Janney touched Ross, needing him, but she was unable to take her eyes from the crazy man's, as if they had entered some sort of juvenile staring contest, and the loser would be food for the winner.

She was able to get air into her mouth and throat, but not into her lungs. Her fingertips against Ross's shoulder became her lifeline. The part of her that faced the crazy man had become a target. A diagram illuminated on an overhead projector, complete with red arrow: Shoot here, right here.

He lifted the rifle, and this time there was absolutely no place to run. No wall to build, no door to slam.

"Kevin. Kevin, what the hell are you up to?"

The duel ended.

His eyes left hers first, turning back toward the house and the man shouting in the yard. Janney saw a pair of figures running across the grass, glistening in the night like joggers decked out in fluorescent strips. The rifle that had been lifted to kill her shot at them instead. One of the figures went down writhing and screaming, and the other shot back.

She could not believe it. Danger coming from two directions at once. The noise the gunfire made was deafening: a great monstrous smashing and clapping, like cracked gongs, as if armies were congregating, instead of three men.

"Back in the sand trap," said Ross quite calmly, as if requesting a glass of lemonade. Janney took the wheelchair and shoved it over the little bluff, and she and Ross fell awkwardly and painfully into the sand. Ross was twisted grotesquely by his fall, the wheelchair half on him and half hooked on a thick tuft of grass above him. Janney began to straighten him out. Once she had the wheelchair off him, Ross pulled himself under the protective two feet of grassy bluff. Janney remained crouched. Her throat hurt. I didn't fall on my throat, Janney thought. Why does it hurt so much? Her throat felt constricted, as if she had a strep infection.

Ross's hand clamped down over her mouth, and suddenly, nightmarishly it was Ross with whom she was struggling. She could not breathe, she could not live—it was Ross who was going to kill her. Oh, God, thought Janney, tears burning her eyes, explain this to me, what is—

"Shut up," Ross whispered fiercely, "stop screaming. Janney, get hold of yourself. Stop screaming!"

He took his hand off her mouth, and the breath she drew in scraped down her raw throat. She swallowed, and that hurt, too.

Kevin leaped into the sand trap with them. The sole of his shoes raked down Janney's bare leg as if he'd given her calf a wrist burn. She fell back against Ross and marveled at how slowly and smoothly Ross's heart was beating. Her own was leaping about erratically, as if trying to escape.

Kevin hit the sand, rolled, holding his rifle up and away from himself, and ended in a prone position with the barrel of the rifle pointing directly at them. He might have been practicing the stunt for weeks, it went so smoothly. And once again their eyes locked.

If Ross had not been there with his fingers curved around her shoulders, hanging onto her, keeping her safe, she could not have faced the crazy man again. Having an ally made a tremendous difference. That's the way *you're* supposed to be, God, she thought. When I walked through the valley of the shadow of death, I wasn't supposed to feel alone. Well, I did.

Janney met the man's eyes—Kevin, the other riflemen had been calling him, Kevin somebody—and from somewhere her mind began playing old theater music: the vamping rhythmic chords of the approaching bad guy.

A smile prickled the corners of her mouth, escaped, and blossomed into a grin, and looking at Kevin, Janney knew that he truly and literally would shove that grin down her throat.

"So," said Ross conversationally, "what's the story here?"

"Shut up," said Kevin equally conversationally, as if Ross had the right to refuse, in which case Kevin would shoot him. "Get away from each other. Laura, move over there." He gestured several feet to the right. When she did not obey, he did something to the rifle that made it click, and the metallic sound was utterly persuasive.

One click, one snap, and he had demonstrated totally that he was in charge. That all Janney could supply was the background music to her own death.

She moved.

Kevin slid forward, rather like a lizard, and with one hand holding the rifle, and his muscular torso propelling him ahead, the other hand lifted the wheelchair up onto the bluff. It was the sort of maneuver that Janney would have considered impossible, and she was impressed when Kevin achieved it without the slightest trouble.

The men in her backyard were yelling at Kevin again. They seemed to have the idea that if everybody were introduced, this whole thing would dissolve into a mere misunderstanding and they all would end up smiling and shaking hands. The men were cops. They kept saying,

"Now, Kevin. Kevin, son." And Kevin, with a noticeable lack of filial feeling, fired at them.

Better them than me, thought Janney. After all, those cops have guns and trees and presumably exits, cars, radios, telephones, and my entire house. I have a lousy sand trap.

She wondered where the golf cart had gone. Wrenching her eyes off Kevin, at whom she had been staring as if he were a rock star and she a worshipful fan, Janney looked behind her. The car was upside down, its motor still purring softly, three of its wheels spinning in midair and the fourth gently digging a hole in the sandy bluff. The pretty sunshade was smashed beneath the metal. Here lies Janney Fraser, she thought.

Kevin was using the wheelchair for protection, shooting from behind it. A few aluminum rods and a leather sling seemed rather meager protection to Janney, but in this case, the more meager, the better.

Kevin jerked the bolt on his rifle, which regurgitated the used cartridge into the sand. The bolt reminded her of one of Donny's toys: long and fat, with a big round black knob no toddler's hand could miss. Kevin moved it with the base of his palm, cupping it slowly, not as if the action were stiff but as if he relished the gesture. After reaching into his pocket, Kevin pulled out several more shells and dropped them into a slot in the rifle. The moonlight winked on them. They bore an eerie resemblance to lipsticks: slender, silvered Art Deco tubes.

The men were exchanging both verbal and physical fire. Janney was unable to follow any of it, as if she were a blind woman at a tennis match. Kevin's feet were only an inch from Ross's. Janney found herself mesmerized by the sight of those four feet. Two were clad in terry-cloth slippers that drooped and filled with sand. Two were covered by ankle-high hiking boots in a rough dark leather with soles too thick ever to wear out and rawhide laces that dangled in the sand like spaghetti.

A bullet went through the sling seat of the overturned wheelchair, regrettably missing Kevin, who ducked back

down into the sand and cursed. Janney flattened herself
even more. Ross merely lay there, as if watching a ball
game on the tube, head on one arm crooked behind him.

"You better forget about shooting back!" yelled Kevin.
"I got a cripple and an old woman down here with me, and
you'll be up for murder yourself, you keeping shooting!"

An old woman, thought Janney. She was incensed. *Old*.
She was *forty*. How dare he call her an old woman? You
and Todd Weathers, she thought. You—you twerps.

For the first time she no longer wanted to run away
from the man. She wanted to defeat him. It was a funny,
bulging feeling, like a suspect can of vegetables.

Janney's fingers closed around the golf ball in her
pocket.

Ross was face-to-face with someone tall, strong, athletic, handsome, muscular—and he felt no envy. I'd rather
be me, thought Ross. Unbelievable.

Janney pressed into him. He held her shoulder, trying
to calm her with his fingers. "It's okay," he breathed in
her ear, "It's okay." He remembered her, six or seven years
ago, sitting by his bed, telling him it was okay. How he'd
hurled books and radios and ashtrays at her for having
the gall to utter those patently untrue syllables.

A strange, brittle grin was jumping around Kevin's
face, as if the man had rusted-out electrical connections
to his lips. Blood had dried below his nose, giving him a
bearded, cooked appearance. The front of his shirt was
stained with blood. The dark brown streaks seemed to be
coming from a wound in the tiny alligator stitched to the
shirt's left front.

"First those cops get theirs," said Kevin. He had a charming voice, the sort that fills morning talk shows. "And
then," he said, smiling a wide, tic-marred smile, "Laura
gets hers." He stroked the barrel of the gun lovingly.

Ross began to understand the metaphor of one's eyes
being riveted to someone else's. Kevin's eyes were soldered
in Janney's direction. Ross he did not bother with. Ross
had been assessed and marked worthless. For once this

did not upset Ross. From a physical sense he was worthless. When he tangled with Kevin, it would have to be mentally. He let Kevin have a staring match with his stepmother and tried to think his way out.

"Laura, you get over there," ordered Kevin.

It was most odd to hear her referred to as Laura. It seemed to place a fourth person in the sand trap, a woman named Laura, whom Ross had never met but whom Kevin obviously hated. Janney crawled backward away from them both, never taking her eyes off Kevin's. They're like animals facing off, thought Ross, like wild dogs sniffing each other.

He did not feel as if his screaming, terrified Janney were there. She had been replaced by an unblinking hard woman named Laura. If it turned out to be true, of course, that adversity strengthened character, one would have to expect that Janney's would be extraordinarily strong. Until now he'd have said that adversity had diluted it.

A silver lining, Ross thought. Neat. I learn to conquer pain. Janney learns to face troubles squarely. And then blast, wham, zap! We get canceled.

"This your boyfriend, this cripple?" Kevin said to Janney.

"He's my son." She said it definitively, with great finality, as if cementing them. Neither Janney nor Ross had ever used the word without the *step*.

"Don't either of you move," said Kevin.

That seemed a simple enough thing for Ross to succeed at.

Kevin crawled all the way down the opposite end of the sand trap and fired from there. There was a yell from the backyard and a throaty chuckle from Kevin. Apparently the cops hadn't believed the line about a cripple and an old woman in the sand trap with Kevin because one of them fired back and the bullet sailed not more than a few inches above Ross's head.

Pain exploded in Ross as if the bullet really had struck him. He chewed on the headache, trying to defeat it, and failed completely. Within moments he was sagging back on the sand, getting himself prone, trying to ease the head-ache out.

He was only remotely aware of Kevin and Janney both crawling back toward him and feeling him for bullet holes. Janney was screaming at the top of her lungs for the cops to stop shooting. "Tell 'em," said Kevin wolfishly. "Tell 'em I'll do all the shooting."

Janney and Kevin had a conversation but Ross could not hear it. All his senses were concentrated on trying to whip the pain.

His stepmother's voice came scratched and out of sync, like an old record played at the wrong speed. "He's absolutely helpless," she was saying to Kevin. "Believe me, he can't hurt you. Ross can't do anything."

Rage hit Ross harder than the pain.

It seemed to start in his capillaries and surge through his arteries and leap in his heart. How dare she? he thought. How dare she tell him I can't do anything?

As suddenly as before, he was climbing above the dizzying pain, circling past it, shelving it.

It's anger, he thought. Anger is the key to whipping the pain. Oh, Janney, ten thousand thanks.

Ross breathed very lightly, assessing himself gingerly, not wanting to rock his boat or his plane or whatever had brought him out of the pain.

Catherine stood hunched and horrified in front of the open trunk of the Cadillac, her husband half in her arms, half on the floor of the trunk. The gunfire ceased. She found she had not breathed during the shooting, and it hurt to release her rib muscles and allow her lungs to inflate again.

Silence filled her more completely than the huge, smashing cracks of the guns: a silence that crept into her mouth and coated her tongue. For some time she remained paralyzed until her bent back began to ache, and the homely, elderly feelings of the backache woke her up.

She had been concentrating so completely on Grey that

the gunfire had shocked her but not made sense to her. Think, she told herself, think!

Thought was beyond her.

The need to be silent, to match the dreadful silence that now surrounded her, gave Catherine a sense of being underwater. Of drowning next to someone who, if she could only mention it, would save her.

Drowning, she thought. Death. Grey. Ambulance.

She sagged, lowering her husband, whispering inarticulate assurances, and tottered the dozen feet or so to the police car to use its radio. "Ambulances," she said to it over and over. "Ambulances."

CHAPTER

SIXTEEN

ED DID NOT WANT TO LOOK DOWN and examine himself. He had both palms pressed down over the hole in his side, and both were getting wet and slippery. His back was up against a railroad tie that formed the side of an untended flower bed. Shasta daisies leaned over him like a funeral bouquet.

Thirty feet away Bob was frozen upright behind a tree trunk. The tree had a large branch sticking out just where Bob needed to be, so Bob was curved around it: safe in his upper and lower regions and vulnerable at the waist. "What the hell is this?" said Bob, sucking in his belly.

"He ain't using tennis balls," said Ed.

"How bad is that wound?"

"Bad." It hurt more at the edges of the wound and less at the center, as was reasonable. Whatever had been at the center no longer existed. Ed could not imagine what had made him rush yelling down the backyard directly into Kevin's fire, trying to scold him as if he were Kevin's Sunday school teacher. I'm retarded, he thought. "It's jist that Ah *know* Kevin," he said irritably to Bob. "Ah mean, yew don't think someone yew *know* is gonna start playing sniper."

"The guy's wanting to kill us both, and your feelings are hurt as much as your stomach," said Bob.

Ed tried to laugh. The pain that came out was unreal. The wound was like a suction cup, pulling all his body, all

157

his attention, into the hole. "Ah wasn't thinkin'," said Ed. "Akshally Ah was gettin hungry and whin th' call came from th' Halfway House, all Ah could think of was Bick's waffles an' a cuppa coffee w' extra cream."

"Beats thinking about Kevin." Bob was trying to bury himself in the bark. He twisted suddenly and shot at Kevin, who shot right back, from a different angle.

There was a paralyzed silence.

"Yew hurt, too?" said Ed.

"Little scrape on my arm. Scared me mostly. Any more room behind that railroad tie? I got to vacate this spot in a hurry. Kevin's shifting position, and I can't."

"Be mah guest."

Bob flung himself forward and hurtled onto the ground below Ed's feet, smashing his elbow on what was, upon examination, weed-covered brick edging where the tie ended. Kevin shot again. Bob stacked the bricks where he hoped they'd be useful.

"Would it be smarter to lie here in silence," said Bob, "or try to talk Kevin into surrendering?"

"He's not goin' tuh surrender," said Ed. "Yo' out a yo' mahnd if yew think he'd surrender."

"We might lie here forever."

"Nah. He'd kill us first."

They heard their radio crackle indistinguishably and a low frantic voice talking into it, equally indistinguishably. "That there lady's cool," said Ed.

Bob began to shout soothingly at Kevin. He did not particularly want other cops to come and find him lying behind a clump of flowers. It would be a lot better if he had Kevin sitting quietly in the Volkswagen by the time Catherine Randallman's reinforcements arrived. "Now, Kevin," he yelled. Unfortunately Kevin interpreted this as an order ("*Now!*") and shot again.

"Ah think Kevin wants he should go down inna blaze a glory," said Ed. "Ain't nothin' gonna make him surrender."

"If he had a brain the size of a pea, he'd get away from here now anyway," said Bob. "He's got the whole damn golf course back there. What the hell's he hanging around for?"

"Killin' his uncle gave him a appetite." Ed was unable to keep a grip on his wound. The blood oozed past his slippery fingers, and the sides of the wound separated. His wife had been in the shower, and the kids asleep, when he'd left for work that evening. Didn't kiss anybody good-bye, thought Ed. He clung to his flesh as if to a life pre-server.

"This is terrific," said Bob gloomily. "You're wounded, and you can't shoot anyway. I'm protected by six old bricks, and I can't even see the golf course through these dumb flowers. Kevin probably figures he's really up against something here. Two officers of the law and so forth."

"Little do he know," whispered Ed.

Kevin's left hand curled gently around the barrel of his rifle, like a violinist waiting out the empty beats. Music to kill by, Janney thought. The rifle had the grace and strength she associated with musical instruments: the lovely smooth curve of the neck of her violin or the ex-quisite polished grain of her grand piano. The rifle is beau-tiful, she thought, astonished. It should be ugly. Utilitarian.

But of course, it was very utilitarian. If you wanted death.

Oh, Lord, how long will you look on? Rescue me from the roaring beasts.

She was swimming in psalms.

And Ross, what was he swimming in? Pain?

Kevin, several yards away, was sighting on the police-men. An expression of almost academic concentration was on his face. He seemed neither grim nor angry, but stu-dious and careful. A man who was going to do something just once and do it right.

Janney swallowed bile.

Ross whispered, "We have to get out of here."

"I've been trying for some time. It isn't as easy as it looks."

Their voices were low and intimate. Janney was reminded of witches muttering over a caldron.

"The element of surprise," said Janney.

But neither of them was able to think of a surprise to reveal.

"The art of distraction," said Ross.

"How," said Janney, "do you distract a madman with a gun and not at the same time tempt the madman to kill you?"

Kevin crawled back toward them. Ross said to him, "You sure got those cops pinned down. They're not going anywhere or doing anything."

"Figured that out all by yourself?" said Kevin contemptuously. He did not even look at Ross. His eyes narrowed at the sight of Janney's bandaged hand.

"They're only police," said Ross. "If they had any real brains, they'd be doing something else."

Kevin took Janney's hand in an almost courtly manner, as if to kiss it.

"I could fire at them," said Ross. "Cover you while you go on down the golf course and get away."

Kevin stared at him.

"I mean it, Kevin. You think I'm fond of cops?"

How clever of Ross, thought Janney. Kevin can't have *meant* to end up here like this. He can't *want* to be caught in a stupid sand trap. He must want to be gone, to be running, to be going wherever he meant to go. All we have to do is offer him a way out.

Kevin ripped the sock bandage off her hand, and the blood oozed again. Janney shuddered, trying to pull her hand back, and Kevin dug thick, dirty fingernails into the wound.

"After all, Kevin, in a little while they'll have more men down here," said Ross. "And when this sand trap is surrounded, I just don't see how you're going to get away. Right now it's still dark, dawn isn't for a while, and there's only those two cops you've got pinned down and one of them is hurt."

"A wimp like you, who can't even hold up his own skull,

is going to cover for me? Nobody'd pay a buck for that joke."

Sirens began to sound in the distance, like whimpering cats. Kevin dropped Janney's hand and crawled back to the edge of the bluff.

Janney found herself beaming with delight. Police. Ambulances. Rescue. Safety.

Janney began to have visions of apartments. Elevators for Ross. City sidewalks. View of skylines instead of golfers. Specifically, a view of Boston's skyline. Somewhere they could survive on Ross's pension and a part-time music income from her. The daydream grew wonderfully, colorfully, and she could hear the music and see the apartment, the nap of the wall-to-wall carpet it would have, the awkwardness of the coat closet, the cramped bathroom that would have a view of—make it a really good daydream—Louisburg Square.

On television, police were either wondrously stupid or magnificently competent. The two in her backyard running right into Kevin's fire, scolding him, introducing themselves, clearly fell into the wondrously stupid category. If life were fair, the next set would be in the magnificently competent range.

"Ambulance," muttered Kevin. "Who the hell called an ambulance?"

His bifocals had been lost somewhere in the shuffle. Grey could see nothing but a series of dark blurs layered on up into a darker sky. He closed his eyes and drifted with his thoughts. He felt if he could keep his thoughts away from death, he might succeed in not drifting in that direction.

He was able to think only of Kevin. Of what had gone wrong.

Mankind still hunts, every one of us, he thought. By television, cheering on the private eye, or by sports, rooting for the team, or by paperbacks, or garage sales, or ambulance chasing. The twentieth-century necessity is passivity. And Kevin lacks it. He has to do his hunting himself.

"But why is Kevin doing this?" Catherine cried out, cradling him. Grey tried to answer her, pleased with his own deductions, but he lacked the strength. He felt himself slipping. It was not as frightening, really, as the heart attack had been.

"Who knows?" said the ambulance attendant. "For kicks maybe."

Grey found it an interesting phrase. Had man once literally hunted by kicks? Stomping on small lizards, treading on baby rabbits?

They were lifting him onto a stretcher, and he felt pain as his folded body was straightened out, but he could not open his eyes to watch. I am dying, he thought.

With Catherine's hand on his forehead and the attendant's on his wrist it seemed a rather safe thing to do. Relaxing, like getting into a hot bath.

Kevin doing his caveman thing. Surviving by killing.

And me, thought Grey, equally uncivilized. Surviving by poisoning my own town.

He did not want to repent before his Maker. He wanted to repent before Holly Oak and make things right, face whatever had to be faced. The last thing Grey Randallman felt was the cool pressure of his wife's fingers and the smooth softness of the stretcher. *Oh, Christ, Catherine, I'm sorry.*

Obviously there was no way he was going to turn his rifle over to anybody, let alone that cripple. Still, the man was right. Kevin had to get moving. There was definitely no future in this sand trap.

Till the nose healed, he'd have to hole up somewhere. Dye his hair. Look different. Pair of glasses maybe. Stay away from the golf and tennis for a while.

Of course, the whole thing would depend on his getting away from the sand trap without the cops realizing that the threat to them had left. He needed the time they'd spend hiding from a gun that was no longer there. Which meant, clearly, that neither Laura nor the cripple could be left able to call out an explanation of what Kevin was doing.

Kevin began to plan a way to kill the man and Laura without the cops sensing that he was doing it. "Laura, old girl," he said. "Dig me a foxhole."

"A what?"

"A foxhole. In the sand. Deep. So I can straighten up a little. I'm getting a backache like this. Right here. Get over here and dig it."

She didn't move.

"Laura, you argue with me, and the first nose to go is your precious son's, got it?"

Jeez, he didn't even need a rifle to threaten Laura. Just her own son. Kevin grinned, watching the woman. She tried scooping up the sand with cupped hands, but the sand was dry, soft, and uncooperative. As fast as she scooped, it slid gently back and reoccupied its chosen space. Kevin encouraged her with quiet threats toward her son. In another minute she was digging like a dog, flinging sand between her legs and behind her, her curved fingers and palms making little shovels. She had to circle her own hole in order to remove the sand evenly and successfully. Her skirt was rather long. Even when her butt was up pretty high, so she could shove the sand between her legs, it draped down to cover her thighs. Eventually she was digging with her butt facing Kevin. The sexual temptation was strong. He knew he couldn't actually rape her and still hang on to the rifle, and the cripple had no legs but he still had arms and would doubtless want to prevent his mother's rape. Kevin could use his hand. That would shake old Laura up a little. Kevin grinned and crawled toward her.

"You do," said the cripple quite clearly, "and I'll shove that rifle up yours."

Laura stopped digging. She was entirely bent over. She regarded them both upside down through the V of her legs.

Kevin tried to laugh at the idea of the cripple's hurting him, but the man's eyes and face were not crippled, and the eyes were glittering, and Kevin knew abruptly that he'd been right after all. It was the man he had to worry about. He had to kill the man first.

He squatted in the sand and faced the man instead of Laura. "Keep digging, Laura," said Kevin. "Unless you want your kid to have three eyes."

He let the ambulance attendant get about halfway down the driveway toward the shouting policemen and then shot at the guy. "Missed him," he said. "Guy all dressed in white like that, how'd I miss?"

It seemed almost comical to Kevin. That guy didn't know how lucky he was. If Kevin hadn't had his mind on other things—stupid Laura, stupid son—that ambulance guy would be dead, dead, dead, because Kevin could hit anything, anytime. "Dead, dead, dead," sang Kevin softly, to the tune of "Three Blind Mice."

The shot had served its purpose. The ambulance guy fled, leaving the cops stranded at the bottom of the yard, and in a moment the ambulance itself left, presumably with Grey's corpse. "Hurry up, Laura," said Kevin.

He looked up at the sky. Good. Another patch of clouds moving in. He didn't need them to kill off this worthless pair, but he did want the moon hidden before actually leaving the sand trap, in case one of those cops was able to see anything.

The man would die first. Kevin would talk about another cop coming and act as if he were going to shoot over the cripple's head, and then he'd just let the cripple have it. Didn't matter if Laura screamed. The cops wouldn't know why she was screaming. And the position he was putting her in, head dipping in and out of the foxhole, he didn't have to shoot Laura. After her son was dead, Kevin would just hold Laura head down, sit on her. Cover her face up with sand. It would be kind of fun. She'd buck like a bronco, trying to get air.

A deep, throbbing excitement filled Kevin. He could not resist watching Laura dig another few seconds. He wondered if there was any sexual satisfaction in dying. Would Laura feel death only in her mouth and lungs and nose? Or would she feel him, riding her the way her husband must have, cock shoving against her ass? He wondered if she would have an orgasm as she died.

Kevin giggled to himself. I will, he thought.

He wondered how to go about getting a false identity. He'd need a driver's license. Not from North Carolina, where they put your photograph on it. New York maybe. Enough people in New York City to blend in with. Social Security number, thought Kevin. Credit cards. He patted his hip to feel his wallet, and it was gone.

Gone! he thought. My goddamn wallet. My money! It must have fallen out in the *sand*. But he had to have that money! Goddamn Laura, she was a jinx, she was evil; if she hadn't driven past, none of this would even have *happened*. He would kill her first after all. The cripple couldn't do anything but yell.

Kevin felt Laura right in his fingernails, felt how her blood and her flesh had been in that cut on her hand, and he thought: I'll rip her apart, that's what I'll do, I'll pull her apart by her goddamned jaws, I'll—

And a van and several cars turned down Mashie Lane.

One thing you learned after helping in a rest home for twenty years was how to take a pulse. Grey's pulse had become more thready, more irregular. Grey was much more religious than Catherine. Happy are those who trust in the Lord, she thought. Let it be, let it be.

The attendants seemed to stroll up to her, seemed to stand next to Grey as if they were cake decorations. "Get the stretcher," she said, filled with a wild, unconquerable anger. "Hurry up! Get the goddamn stretcher!"

Catherine Randallman had never uttered a swear word in her life. She said things like *darn* or *sugar* because they were, as her grandmother had explained fifty-odd years ago, banana peelers for *damn* and *shit*. "Damn it," she said to the ambulance attendants, "don't be so slow, you stupid southerners."

But it no longer mattered.

It didn't matter what she said or who they were.

Grey was dead.

Catherine walked into Janney Fraser's house. She did not turn on the lights but stood quietly in the living room, letting her eyes get used to the dark. The living room was curiously and badly arranged, with furniture clinging to the walls and a huge concert grand piano and stacks of messy music taking up a third of the room. The telephone was on an incredibly small table, possibly meant for a fern stand. Catherine telephoned the state troopers. During the call she watched the ambulance pull away. Without the desperate wounded policeman. With Grey's body.

"We're already on the way," said the officer. "We got a transmission from Shearing already that he thought he'd need help, and when you started calling for ambulances awhile ago, we picked that up. Sounded like the sort of situation where you could use some more men."

There was no chair next to the telephone. It seemed impossible to Catherine that anyone could live here comfortably. She picked up the phone and walked unsteadily several feet to the nearest chair. It was too large. It was for a big man, not a small woman. Her feet dangled. She told the officer about Kevin. All about him. From the collie dying all those years ago to Rory and Grey.

"And would he?" said the policeman on the phone.

"Would he what?"

"Shoot a woman and a cripple."

The room felt as if it were made up of objects belonging to other people: the furniture on loan, the pictures from the library. Only the piano and the music belonged. That was the only space anybody really used. "Yes," said Catherine. "He would."

"My God," screamed the cop into the phone. "If you knew he was this crazy before, why didn't you do something?"

Grey is dead, she thought. He is actually dead. I was too slow. I was too late.

She listened to the engines of several vehicles turn the corner down Mashie Lane. The reinforcements that would take Kevin as if he were a fox for hounds.

"Because," she said, "I thought Kevin was only a little bit crazy."

The moon slid behind the cloud that Kevin had been counting on, but the cars approaching had their high beams on. Six. One van and five cars. Now, thought Kevin, I've got to run now.

But if he went now, it would be flight. It would be a chase. It would be Kevin scrambling instead of the police. To run now would be running in fear instead of victory.

He tried to think clearly and make his decision fast. Kill them quick and run? Or—

A huge spotlight suddenly, terrifyingly, focused on the golf course and swiveled slowly until it glared right on them, directly at the remains of the overturned wheelchair and into the sand trap-itself.

The chance to run was gone.

CHAPTER
SEVENTEEN

THE AMPLIFIED VOICE startled all three of them severely.

"Kevin?" it said.

Ross was still lying with his head slightly propped up by his elbow right under the bluff. Janney had crept up next to him, now that the foxhole, completely exposed, was not going to do Kevin much good. Kevin scurried down the pit several yards and lay prone and sideways against the two or so feet of sand that shaded him from the glare of the spotlight.

"Kevin, I wonder if we could talk things out here," said the voice. "We've got a problem, but I think we can figure a way around it."

All three of them laughed: Janney in hysteria, Ross in cynicism, and Kevin in contempt. We look like people on a picnic, thought Janney.

Legs spread, shoulders slouched, as if we're waiting for the potato chips to be passed.

"Now, Kevin, my name's Chuck, and I'm a friend. We want to sort of wrap this thing up without anybody else getting hurt. Okay? Right?"

Avery, thought Janney. That's Avery's double out there, Chuck. Cheerleading his way through quicksand.

"Kevin, I want you to listen carefully to this. Your uncle is still alive. That's why the first ambulance rushed off so fast. If Mr. Randallman gets to the hospital in time, you

169

won't be facing a murder charge. Think about it, Kevin. I know you're fond of your uncle. It was all an accident. Things just happened a little too fast for everybody, I guess. You want to come and talk about it with me? How's that sound?"

"Sounds like shit," said Kevin to Janney and Ross. "I shot half his chest away. They just want to sneak over here and get their cops out."

Mr. Randallman? thought Janney. Grey?

But he was a lovely man. A teddy bear sort of man. Huggy. She'd always wanted to be married to a squeezable sort of man like Grey Randallman. Kevin was his nephew. Kevin had shot half his chest away. Kevin had—

She moaned. "I saw it, didn't I?" she whispered.

Kevin looked at her. "On top of everything else, Laura," he said, "you're stupid. Why did you think I went after you anyway?"

"I didn't know. I couldn't figure it out." She was weeping, loudly, horribly, for Grey Randallman. God, it was just like Donny. A good person. A person the world needed.

"Kevin?" said Chuck's huge, vibrating voice. "Hey, Kevin? Are you okay? You're not hurt, are you?"

"No, man," yelled Kevin. "I'm not hurt. I'm *doing* the hurting."

"Now, Kevin, there's no percentage in thinking like that. The trouble is deep enough already. We can still work out deals, Kevin, but not if you keep making threats. Are Mr. and Mrs. Fraser all right?"

"Listen," said Kevin to Ross, "you guys mother and son or husband and wife or what?"

"Mrs. Fraser is my stepmother," said Ross.

Janney put herself on an airplane for Logan. Or a train, leaving from Fayetteville. For that matter, a Greyhound, leaving from anywhere. In a minute it'll be over, she told herself. We'll be safe. She listened to Chuck talk about surrender. Chuck had about as much chance of accomplishing that, she thought, as Avery did of making Ross walk again.

Chuck's the one who's crazy. And me, too, I'm crazy. As

if Kevin would surrender. He doesn't have a surrendering bone in his body. We are in this to the finish, and the finish is going to be very bloody.

She forced herself not to cry anymore.

Tears would only drip in the sand.

She had to think, figure a way out of this.

To solve a problem, you reduced it to its smallest parts. Small parts. There had to be something. There had to be some tiny thing she could use to win.

But everything had already been reduced to its smallest parts. Sand. Grass. A gun.

"Listen, Kevin, I know you must be pretty hungry." Chuck had his mouth pressed against the microphone. They could hear his lip and tongue noises and the suck of air filling his lungs. "We're having ourselves something to eat up here, and we'd be glad to get you something, too. We've brought along some food and some Pepsi. You thirsty? I've got Coke, too, if you like that better."

How southern, thought Janney. The first thing they do in a hostage situation is offer an assortment of soda pop, they're so sure nobody can exist without a daily dose of cola. Cola drinkers had a sort of party loyalty. There were the RC folks, the cherry cola supporters, the Pepsi fans, and the Coca-Cola aficionados. It did not surprise Janney in the least when Kevin muttered that the only thing he liked to drink was Dr Pepper.

"Tell Chuck," said Janney. "I'm sure he'll get it for you. Tell him to make mine Mello Yello."

"Shut up."

Janney tried to find her daydream again and bury herself in it, but her thoughts wavered and disappeared.

"They're in your house," said Kevin, as if the trespass of it scandalized him. "They're upstairs in that empty bedroom."

"You were in my upstairs?" said Janney. *You were in the empty rooms?* You were in—

He had been in Donny's room.

But it isn't Donny's, she thought. It isn't anybody's. If

Kevin can walk there, it isn't anything to me. Donny is dead. That room, that house, they're no good.

Kevin sidled backward under the bluff until he got to the protection of the golf cart. He aimed higher than before, and she could actually hear the bullet break the window. Mixed in with the awful bang was a gentle tinkle of breaking glass, like a triangle trying to be heard over a full orchestra.

It's the house, she thought. That's half our problem, that stupid house. The location is terrible. Cost of utilities insufferable. Mortgage impossible. I can't sell the thing, but where is it written that I have to be chained to Avery's house and Avery's mortgage and Avery's decorator furniture? It's in Avery's name. Let it rot in Avery's name.

She felt almost triumphant after the decision to take Ross and forget about Holly Oak. No music came to her mind. Perhaps the sight of Kevin, maddened, was too basically unmelodious for music.

Kevin stopped shooting and scuttled back to them. Sinking down in the safety of the grassy overhang, he watched her. He's going to smash my nose first, she thought, and then kill me. A nose for a nose. Kevin is very Old Testament.

For my life is wasted with grief and my years with sighing.

Ah, dumb woman, she thought. Now, when you want to pick up the pieces and keep going, Kevin's going to splinter them into fragments so small they can't be swept up.

Nobody fired back at Kevin. He fired again and then had to drop more shells into his rifle. He continued to remind her, grotesquely, of Donny. Donny dropping pennies between the piano keys. Kevin dropping shells into the rifle. The same intent pleasure in a tiny, repetitive maneuver.

"Kevin?" said Ross.

"Yeah."

"How come you have so much ammunition? Did you know there was going to be a war?"

Kevin slumped against the concave sand bluff. "It's Saturday night," he said. "Or it was."

He offered no more than that. Perhaps Kevin's idea of Saturday night was not a heavy date or a drive-in movie, but a shoot-out.

From beyond the sand trap came a rustling like an army of cicadas or a biblical swarm of locusts. Men, thought Janney, reinforcements, closing in. The gathering of the troops.

It was not comforting. It merely placed her between even more maddened sharpshooters.

"I was going up Randolph County way," said Kevin. "We have some property up there. You can hunt on your own property. I mean, not legally, not right now, deer, that is, but they don't bother you that much. I was going to spend the night in the truck and go hunting early Sunday morning. Spend the whole day hunting. I love to hunt."

There was a long pause.

Janney felt oddly heavy, as if her seven overweight pounds had multiplied cruelly. It was impossible that she would ever do anything again but lie here, making a dent in the sand.

Kevin was obviously unaccustomed to losing. You would expect someone to whom winning is so important to handle things in a winning manner, thought Janney. Kevin has been stupid.

She tried to graph stupidity and losers on a curve with brains and winners, but she was too slow-witted to visualize the correlation. She pressed her cut hand between her knees to ease the pain.

"It's Sunday morning," said Kevin. He laughed shrilly. "And I'm hunting."

She was in shock. She had seen enough people in grief at the old folks' home to know shock. She had not known, however, that you could be aware of your own state of shock and go right on staying in shock.

Here she was in a stranger's kitchen, preparing coffee and heating frozen breakfast buns for policemen, and Grey was dead and going alone to a morgue, and she was not crying for him or for herself, but measuring water for the percolater.

Because of Kevin, she thought. Because Kevin did this, and Kevin's still doing it. I have to help stop him.

Help? she thought. I? Catherine Randallman? When have I ever done anything right?

She moved blurrily through the kitchen, watching her own firm hands distribute coffee to nervous cops, thinking: Grey is dead, thinking: What will I tell the children?, thinking: Is it my fault?

"How did you get here so quickly?" she said to the sheriff. He took cream and sugar. She could not believe that with Grey dead and Kevin insane and keeping hostages and shooting the entire sky out, they were putting cream and sugar in their coffee. They should at least drink it black. We're all insane, she thought.

"You called us," he told her. "You got on that radio and said 'ambulances' about fifty times. What with Kevin Clary's wallet at the Halfway House, and blood on the floor, and Mrs. Fraser's car over by the church and the vandalism there—we-ell, it seemed like we ought to hustle on over."

He pronounced *ambulance* country style: *amby-lance,* rhyming with *dance.* Catherine wanted to correct him. When he said *siren* and pronounced it *sireen,* it seemed almost more important to correct him than to worry about Grey.

Grey is dead, she thought, trying to absorb such an idea. He died in a car trunk. Like a dog hit by a car and left at the side of the road. Grey is dead.

She began crying, quietly, with her back to the policemen.

"Sir," said a young one, much too young to be anything, and yet in uniform, with a holster and a gun in the holster, and a little black plastic sign below his name tag that said "SHARPSHOOTER."

"Yeah?"

"From the upstairs window in the empty bedroom, we

can look down on them, but they're all jammed in together. We can't tell who's who."

"We gotta get some light shining on 'em then," said the sheriff. They began talking about Kevin as if Catherine were personally responsible for him. As if he were a dog whose mistress had neglected to get it rabies shots and now he was rabid and foaming at the mouth and biting innocent people and it was all her fault.

And maybe it was.

"Got to run out of ammunition pretty soon, way he's shooting," said the young one.

"Why you think he has so much?"

"Maybe he was going after squirrels or something?"

"A thirty-ought-six is kind of heavy weather for squirrels."

"Thing is, how do we know when Kevin's out? I don't want to stroll into the backyard if there's a chance he still has one bullet left."

Oh, Grey, how can I handle anything without you? How could you let Kevin kill you? Oh, Grey, don't be dead!

"Don't look at me. I never volunteer for anything."

They snickered, like children, and left Catherine sitting on the floor, wrapped in oak cabinets, drinking her coffee and thinking about death.

Somehow, since they'd been talking, even joking, Bob had figured Ed was not seriously hurt. He hadn't looked at the wound, and anyway, it was too dark to examine bullet holes. The spotlight bathed Ed and Bob in a greenish glow. Bob stared in horror at the red slime that was protruding from Ed's abdomen. "Ed," he whispered.

There was no answer.

Got to tie it up, thought Bob. Get it bound together so it doesn't all fall out or get on the ground and get dirty.

Kevin had two shooting angles which had not, so far, varied: behind the wheelchair and behind the golf cart. Bob wondered how much easier it would be for Kevin to shoot with the light showing him Bob's back. He told himself Kevin wouldn't dare peer above the little bluff anymore, that his back was safe.

Squirming, digging his heels into the ground, and arching his back, he managed to remove his shirt. After sliding forward to Ed's side, Bob began to wrap the shirt around Ed. He worked it under Ed's ribs and around the other side, under the left arm and back to meet the other end of shirt when he realized that Ed was dead.

For a long moment Bob just lay there, staring into the wound that was no longer bleeding. Then he tied the shirt anyway, covering up the intestines, smoothing the fabric over the congealing blood.

Oh, Kevin, man, I'm going to get you, thought Bob Shearing. His anger came in a rainbow, reds and oranges and yellows of wrath ripping through him and ending up in his right hand.

He'll be looking at the van and the spotlight, Bob thought. I'll crawl up the far end and use the opposite side of the golf cart for cover. Get the bastard right in the face.

The colors were still in him, like broken prisms, stabbing him with fury. He got up and ran swiftly into the thick shielding shrubbery on the opposite side of the Frasers' lawn, and nobody shot or yelled at him.

"You know what Avery would say about this?" murmured Ross.

They lay almost companionably watching Kevin's antics. He reminded Ross of Donny when too much was going on and he was the center of attention or when he failed to get his nap. Bouncing from room to room, priming himself for even more wild behavior. Except that Donny had had plastic toys and Kevin had a very real rifle.

"What?"

"He'd say, 'don't lie there pretending to be helpless! Look upon this as a challenge!'"

They choked on laughter. It was as if Avery, with his pet phrases and instant slogans, were standing on the green, doing cheerleading routines with a golf club.

"T-s-i-a-j," said Janney.

"Huh?"

"T-s-i-a-j."

"Do you wish to elaborate on that, or do I make up my own interpretation?"

"It's a chamber work by Charles Ives. *TSIAJ*. 'This scherzo is a joke.'" Janney began laughing out loud.

Kevin came back toward them in the sort of crab walk children master to win ribbons on Field Day. It was a dreadful posture, as if he were some great insane spider, with a deep hairy maw and poisonous fangs. Ross and Janney both shrank into the sand.

"Laughing?" said Kevin between his teeth. "At me?"

From somewhere a damp breeze tossed a dry leaf along the sand trap. It moved gently, almost poetically, in front of Kevin, and fluttered. Kevin stomped on the leaf as if it were a rodent. His knee, doubled under his chin, had a bizarre condensed strength, as if what they had thought was merely a stick had turned out to be a powerful piston.

Oh God, thought Ross, the laughter in him drying up permanently. We can't possibly outfight Kevin. And even if we outthink him, Kevin will still be equipped with a rifle. He'll still be stronger, speedier, and in a lot more trouble. Mind over matter, thought Ross, remembering Peter's admonitions. Bunch of shit. What matters is, Kevin is strong and we are weak.

For the second time Kevin took Janney's hand and looked down into the cut and smiled. It was a nice smile. In fact, a lovely smile. Bet his parents think he can do no wrong, thought Ross.

If I could jam sand into the barrel, it'd explode, thought Ross. He'd gone hunting once and a wasp flew into the barrel of his .22, and the next time he fired, expecting the unfortunate wasp to be hurled out, the barrel had exploded on him.

Or even a few grains of sand might do it. Slow the action certainly. Maybe stop the automatic altogether.

But what if the rifle were next to his stepmother's face when it exploded?

He tried to decide if he and Janney had enough strength

and foolhardiness to grab the rifle and just shove it muzzle down into the sand and hold it there while screaming for help. Help which was, infuriatingly, just yards away. Kevin, he thought, would be just as glad to kick them to death as shoot them.

The smile on Kevin's face seemed to grow cancerously, absorbing all his other features. With the happy look of a child building a beach castle, Kevin took a handful of sand and drizzled it into Janney's open cut. He jammed his thumb into the raw flesh and rotated it.

Janney jerked and screamed, trying to kick Kevin off, but she was prone and helpless.

Kevin took the edges of the wound and ripped them apart.

Janney's scream turned her face into a gargoyle.

If they'd taught me to hate the Cong like this, I'd have killed the whole army, thought Ross. He launched himself at Kevin: fingers, teeth, and fists. The three of them were attached like hydra, shrieking, salivating, and panting.

Vaguely Ross heard the police yelling Kevin's name. "Kevin, no! Don't make things worse! Don't hurt Mrs. Fraser!" Janney was screaming like a siren, or perhaps it was a siren screaming, and he himself was grunting and huffing like a wild boar.

Kevin pulled free of Ross and hit him on the jaw with the butt of the rifle. The only thing that saved Ross from being decapitated was that Kevin had so little swing space. Through a sea of pain, Ross listened to Janney scream on and on, like aftershocks. He did not lose consciousness. He hung onto the rim of it, as if by his fingernails. Lost my legs, he thought. Now my jaw.

Janney's scream faded. She was cradling his head in her lap.

There had been sirens after all. Their wailing diminished like sea gulls flying away and then stopped. There were more people there for Kevin to scream at, and there seemed to be an entire crowd exchanging epithets.

Ross tried to speak but could not move his jaw.

Janney was crooning to him, rocking him. Being tossed like that was agonizing, but he sensed that she was rocking herself as well, and possibly Donny, and he let her go on.

CHAPTER
EIGHTEEN

KEVIN FIRED AGAIN, very rapidly, and had to reload, and he fired once more. Beethoven, thought Janney. Definitely Beethoven. Theme and variations. And variations. And variations. Sort of your basic Beethoven motif to all this, too. Dum, dum, dum, daaa.

She could not believe how much her hand hurt. She had thought for a moment that Kevin would separate her into halves, starting with her hand and ripping until she split up the middle.

She watched him shoot. The gun literally spit. The cartridges flew up a few inches and then fell into the sand to gleam like glass on a beach, waiting for a child to scoop them up as treasures.

The silence after the crash of firing added importance to the little mechanical slides and clicks of the rifle being readied for another shot. The sounds could have been almost anything—a lock snapping, a door closing, a knob clicking—but they were a gun.

How tiny the actual bullets must be. The cases that dropped were so long. It seemed absurd to be so terribly afraid of such a small bit of metal.

She feared Kevin's hands more than his rifle. She did not know why Kevin had not shot them yet. Was her fantasy right? Would he actually try to kill them with his bare hands?

She shuddered and splinted her hand and told herself the police would succeed any minute now.

Chuck's voice was less good old boy and more nervous job applicant. "Kevin?" he called dubiously.

Kevin did not answer. He was patting his pockets. He pulled out the two shell boxes, which opened for him like the tiny drawers of old-fashioned stick matches. He slid the clear plastic covers off several times, a confused, betrayed expression on his face.

"Mrs. Fraser?" yelled Chuck.

She debated answering. But she could think of nothing to say. "Hello" seemed faintly ridiculous, as did "Yes, Chuck?" or "Still alive." In fact, "Still alive" seemed a remark that would tempt Kevin a bit too much.

"Mr. Fraser? Ross?"

Ross shifted off her lap back into the sand, moaning faintly. Janney seemed to be in pieces. There was a piece of hand in her lap and a piece of brain in her skull. Ross put his hands up and held the lower half of his face. Chuck's hesitant calling ended. Janney tried to find her daydream again and bury herself in it, but it wavered and disappeared.

"All okay?" said Chuck. "Anybody hurt over there?"

Anybody hurt, thought Janney. She breathed in Ross's ear, "Kevin's on his last round."

Ross's eyes opened wide. Through clenched teeth he whispered back, "You sure? One shot left?"

"No. A whole round. He put in five and shot one. Four left."

"A round is only one shot."

"Are you sure?" *Round* sounded plural to Janney. Like *herd* or *flock*. Round.

"Trust me. Round equals one. He's got four left? You positive?"

She did not have to verify it. Kevin crushed the shell boxes in his fist as if they were alive and he were strangling them. Yes, he was at the end. Four shots left.

Ross held onto his jaw and addressed Kevin. "Listen," he said. "You need to do some negotiating. We'll help you.

We're your ticket out of here, Kevin. You need us. Tell them to get you a car and some money. They won't fire on you or stop you if you have us."

Janney had a ludicrous vision of Kevin using Ross as protection. Rebuilding the ruined wheelchair maybe? Or carrying Ross, infant style, in his arms, while keeping the rifle trained on Janney? Perhaps Kevin should negotiate for a new wheelchair while he was at it. The Veterans Administration might cough one up.

She felt anger at Ross for suggesting something that would only extend their nightmare. Kevin had but four shells left. How long, after all, could he go on holding off the veritable army which had encircled them?

The sun was rising. The eastern sky was turning pale gray, like watered silk. Threads of yellow and pink spidered the horizon.

Kevin's nerves were hanging out like the guts of an animal run over by a car.

The tic in his cheek was back, throbbing as if the cheek were chewing its own gum.

He slithered toward the golf cart, got halfway there, and shot at the cart itself, once. There was a grunt from beyond the cart and silence. Janney could not see what Kevin had shot at. Kevin remained slouched in the sand, his eyes swiveling like those of an insect on stalks, looking in all directions with queer, glittering eyes.

Three left, thought Janney, her heart lifting. And we're into the home stretch, pounding around the curve, cheering the winner on.

Winner, she thought. Kevin is a winner. How's he going to win? How's he going to get out of this?

"Kevin, you're completely surrounded," said the voice, losing patience. Chuck was no longer amplified. He was screaming, angry, and tired. "There's no point to all this, Kevin. You're only hurting a lot of innocent people."

She knew horribly, deeply, that the innocent people were going to include Janney and Ross Fraser. Because Kevin had to win. No matter what, he would have to go out on a victory.

Kevin lay in the sand, stroking his rifle, polishing it with his shirttail.

"I haven't resolved any of my religious problems," she whispered to Ross.

He actually grinned. "One doesn't, usually."

"How bad does your jaw hurt?"

"Pretty bad. How's your hand?"

"Still attached."

Ross smiled again. His cheek was scarlet and raw, as if the gun had sunburned it. "You're tough, lady," he said softly.

"I am?" she said.

The eastern sky turned gaudily pink. Wonderful warm pinks and yellows like a happy child's watercolor filled their view. Donny had painted exclusively in red. He had no use for other colors, wouldn't even learn their names. Red's enough, he said firmly.

"What's it like?" said Ross.

"What's what like?"

"That Charles Ives piece. 'This scherzo is a joke.'"

"Oh. Like sand in an open wound."

"Hey. Sounds neat."

"It is, actually. Dreadful when it's happening, but so quirky and interesting you almost want an encore. Not quite, though. You never quite want an encore of Charles Ives."

They watched the day unfold.

"It must be true," she said.

"What?"

"Full moons."

"What about them?"

"People are crazy during full moons. Look at Kevin. A genuine lunatic. Featuring both the tic and the luna."

Ross disagreed. "The only thing I attribute to the full moon is light. If it were pitch-black out here, half of this would never have happened."

"I can prove it scientifically. Now that day is here, Kevin's calm."

"He isn't calm. He's exhausted. His nerves are shot to hell."

Janney watched the bruise rise on her stepson's cheek. "I'm thirsty," she said.

"I wonder just how they planned to deliver those Cokes they brought along."

"Only three bullets left. Maybe we'll find out soon." With her good hand Janney covered a shivery smile lest Kevin see it. "Or maybe we'll be drinking heavenly ambrosia next."

"Speaking of problems not resolved," said Ross suddenly, "it's my fault Donny died, and I'm—I'm sorry."

She stared at him. There was so much pain on his face it was not possible to know which came from Kevin's blow and which from memory. "Your fault?" she said numbly.

"He asked me to play with him and I didn't. He ran out into the road when I could have been playing with him."

"Oh, Ross!" She began crying, kissing him. "Ross, Donny asked me to bake cookies with him and I didn't. He asked Virginia Schmidt to give him a Popsicle and she didn't. It isn't your fault, Ross, honey. It isn't my fault either."

Her words seemed to pass back and forth between them over and over, as if they were a valley and her words an echo. *It isn't my fault either.* Her tears dropped gently on Ross's battered face, and she said, disbelieving, "Oh, Ross, it happened. Oh, God. I'm shriven. I'm done. I'm not guilty."

He touched her, and she thought: He's shriven, too. Why didn't I realize half his problem wasn't Avery, wasn't Vietnam, wasn't illness? It was Donny. Why didn't I see how much guilt we were sharing? Why in God's name *didn't* we share?

Her tears stopped slowly. She began to feel well. Healthy. Whole. Even the throb of her torn hand eased. If I could just lose that seven pounds, she thought, all would be right with the world. Maybe I already lost some of it, what with running around and being under such extreme tension and stress.

She saw herself in an aspirin ad, extolling the virtues of Bufferin for the hostage victim. She saw the glass of water for washing the aspirin down, and her mouth and throat and tongue began to hurt with thirst.

Ross felt almost giddy. He felt as if the burden of Donny's death had floated away, were smiling at him, had absolved him. I can live again, he thought. It would even be worth it.

I've got to make friends with Kevin. I can't let him use those last three bullets. Three is a little too close for comfort. Janney, Ross, and Kevin. It fits a bit too well. If I can just ease Kevin along, maybe I can get him to surrender.

"Kevin?" he said. "What was that shiny car in the driveway?"

"It's commonly known as a police vehicle."

"No, the one that you drove. Looked like an operating table."

"Oh. My uncle's car. It's a 'fifty-seven Fleetwood El Dorado Brougham. Has a brushed stainless steel roof."

"I've never seen anything like that," said Ross. "Hell to refinish if it gets a scratch, huh?"

"You haven't seen anything like that because they made only seven hundred of 'em. Cost Grey thirteen thou brand-new, and that was long before inflation. Year I was born."

Cars, he'll talk cars with me. And I haven't let myself think about cars since I lost the ability to drive them. Seven years. My trivia quotient hovers around zero. Why can't he want to talk radio? I could talk Jean Shepherd and Bernard Meltzer all night. "For that," he said, "your uncle could have bought a Corvette and a Porsche both."

"Yeah, and 'fifty-seven would have been a terrific year to buy a Corvette. That's the classic year. I'd love to have a 'fifty-seven Vette."

Ross struggled to remember anything at all about Corvettes.

"My father used to have a Henry J," said Janney.

Kevin and Ross both ignored her.

"And I learned to drive on an Edsel," she added.

"You still own it?" Kevin asked her, interested.

"No. My parents sold it the year they bought it. They were embarrassed to be seen driving it."

Almost there, thought Ross. Almost relaxed enough to bring up the topics. If only I weren't so tired. And talking hurts so damn much.

From behind the amplified speaker came a woman's voice. It was a thin antique voice, as if the lady talking were very old and wizened.

"Kevin, honey, it's Aunt Catherine," said the voice. "Please, please don't hurt anybody else. We love you, Kevin, we'll help you get through everything. Nobody wants to hurt you. Please, Kevin? Answer me? Please?"

Kevin coiled like a snake, and hatred came out of him like venom from fangs. Ross shuddered.

"Kevin, dear?" croaked the old woman.

Kevin's eyes glittered. Oh, God, no, thought Ross. He's ready to shoot again. Please, God, let him shoot the voice and not Janney or me.

He tried desperately to think of some way, any way, to stop Kevin from killing any more, but there was not one. Kevin's strength had returned, and with it his wrath, and there would be no rescue, not from Ross or anybody else. Ross's daydream that he, Ross, would manage the rescue dissolved. It was like the end of a wonderful movie when there is only the torn theater seat and a greasy popcorn box.

His eyes met Kevin's, and they locked stares. The tic in Kevin's cheek had vanished. If he was crazy still, he was in charge of it; he could do whatever he wanted. Ross's fingers turned cold against his damaged jaw. Ten little ice cubes pressing his bruised flesh. Shoot at the voice, prayed Ross.

But their little war had shrunk back down to three again. Kevin was going to shoot Ross.

Ross was flooded with thoughts: making peace with Donny and God and Avery and Janney and war and presidents and—

Janney began moaning. "No, Kevin," she moaned, "no, oh, please, Kevin, no!" She slid to him imploringly, weep-

ing, and she embraced Kevin's knees and began to kiss
the fair hairs that covered Kevin's long, slim bare calves.
Her lips moved up and down his legs, and her hands stroked,
and out of her mouth came little loving, whimpering sounds,
and Kevin smiled.

Ross was nauseated. How could she *do* that? How could
she possibly kiss the man who had hurt them so much?
Better just to be shot than to submit like that. She was
literally genuflecting. Rubbing her face against Kevin,
begging.

Whether we live or die, Ross thought, Kevin has won.
He brought Janney to her knees. And I, who have to ride
on Janney's actions, I, too, am defeated.

Kevin's gaze met Ross's. Kevin's eyes were sparkling
with triumph—as if all the killing and shooting and agony
and fear had been worthwhile just to have this woman
groveling in supplication.

Ross waited to be shot while Janney kissed his murderer, but Kevin changed position yet again. He would kill
Janney first. Kill her even as she hugged his ankles. She
would be a trophy at his feet.

He could not get to Kevin in time to help his stepmother.
He lacked the adrenaline, the ability, the time: everything.
Kevin guided the barrel of the rifle toward the nape of
Janney's neck. He could buy her only one or two seconds
of life, distracting Kevin, and he did not know if those two
seconds would be worth living, the way she was on her
knees in front of Kevin, groveling.

But he would have to try.

Ross rolled. "Police!" he screamed. "Come on! Now!" He
aimed himself for Janney, the pain in his jaw a boulder
of agony that struck him with every roll. He succeeded in
one thing at least: Kevin shifted his aim to Ross.

Janney jerked violently upright with a thrust of her
shoulder blades that caught Kevin under the chin. She
crashed into him with a bone-snapping jar, and the rifle
spun across the sand. Ross lurched, thinking, *If I could
just get that first!* but Kevin was back on his feet, Kevin

would have the rifle before Janney could turn around, before Ross could roll an inch—

But Kevin did not take a single step.

With a stunned expression on his face Kevin tumbled to the ground. There had been no gunfire. He was not shot. Kevin writhed on the sand like Ross, like some crippled animal. It was almost more nightmarish than anything else to have Kevin scrabbling awkwardly in the sand, leg-less, paralyzed, like Ross.

It was Janney who almost calmly got the rifle and climbed safely out of the sand trap.

"But—but what happened?" said Ross.

The police were trussing Kevin like a turkey. Kevin was truly mad, rabid, spit appearing at the corners of his mouth, screams of rage toward Janney pouring from him like lava.

"Why couldn't he walk?" said Ross. "Why didn't he just take two steps and pick the rifle up?"

"I wasn't kissing him," said Janney. "You didn't think I would really kiss his nasty insane legs, did you?"

Ross stared at her. "You did a good imitation."

"I was merely covering up my other activities." Janney grinned as if she'd conquered the world.

"What other activities?"

"I knew it had to be something little, you see," said his stepmother. "I knew it was just a matter of reducing things to their smallest parts."

She grabbed a Coke from one of the policemen and helped Ross take a swallow. Two men shifted Ross easily and gently from the sand to a stretcher. *"What?"* said Ross. "What did you *do?*"

"I tied his shoelaces together."

Ross began to laugh. Pain shot through his jaw and up into his head, and he laughed again when the doctor jabbed him with morphine. Kevin Clary, with his rifle and his strength and his pride, defeated by a knot in his rawhide laces. "How—how *female* of you," said Ross.

* * *

The sun had risen. The pinks and yellows were gone from the sky. It was going to be a scorching day—blue and blinding white, the Carolina colors. "You want some help, Mrs. Fraser?" said one of the policemen. "Or can you make it?"

Janney looked at the house and the sky and Ross being slid into the ambulance, already asleep, already out of pain and fear. She took a Coke for herself. "I guess," she said, "I guess I can make it."